The Maypole

Geraldine McCaughrean was born in Enfield, north London in 1951. She has a degree in Education from Christ Church College, Canterbury. Her previous books include *A Little Lower Than the Angels*, the winner of the 1987 Whitbread Children's Novel Award, and *A Pack of Lies*, the winner of the 1989 Guardian Award for Children's Fiction. She lives in Oxfordshire.

For Children

One Thousand and One Arabian Nights
The Canterbury Tales
A Little Lower Than the Angels
El Cid
A Pack of Lies

GERALDINE McCAUGHREAN

The Maypole

Geraldine McCaughrean

with best wishes

Secker & Warburg · Minerva

A Minerva Paperback

THE MAYPOLE

First published in Great Britain 1989
by Martin Secker & Warburg
This Minerva edition published 1990
by Secker and Warburg · Mandarin
Michelin House, 81 Fulham Road, London SW3 6RB

Minerva is an imprint of the Octopus Publishing Group

Copyright © Geraldine McCaughrean 1989

ISBN 0 7493 9041 7
A CIP catalogue record for this title
is available from the British Library

Printed in Great Britain
by Cox & Wyman Ltd, Reading

For David Calder

Day came in like Joshua, with ramshorn blasts of sun, but left dark rubble hills standing round the town casting their long, breeched darknesses across the buildings. The hilltop monastery stood smugly aloof in its own pre-ordained sunlight, and monks, flapping like white flags in the wind, were already surrendering themselves to the day's work – fetching cows in from the heath, digging inside the picket, tending yellow raffia hives.

In the village, three or four housewives came to their doors to empty the night's water into the street. They stayed to watch the uric puddles of sunlight trickle into standing pools of yellow. The sun pulled life out of the houses as arduously as it pulls maggots out of discarded meat.

Black motish flies spiralled away from a clatter of shutters. A young woman, her face and smock pleated with sleep, looked out at the street and the heath beyond it. A voice from inside said, 'Where's your modesty? Fetch yourself in, you slut. Showing yourself off.' But the girl stayed by the window. Her eye was caught by a movement near the monastery fishpools. Perhaps it had been the morning's first glitter in the two grey eyes of water. No, a moment later she made out the shapes of two men walking towards town, heavily muffled up in cloaks. One was carrying a bag of some sort. As they passed behind chestnut thickets, newly kindling in the sunlight to a fiery red, the other unfastened his cloak and carried it over his arm, turning his face upwards to warm it. His hair caught the light like the goldwork on some white and brown heraldic beast rampant against a field of crimson bars.

A clove-sized head appeared over the picket of the monastery garden, disappeared again. Then a monk, clutching up his skirts, ran round from behind the fence. He shouted and pointed after the two men who abruptly broke into a run and ducked off the track into the thicket.

The outraged monk seemed not to know whether a chase was worthwhile. He consulted with two more gardeners, pointing first at the ponds and then in the direction of the poachers. A bell began chinking dully inside the monastery tower; the three looked towards the noise like playing children called indoors.

'Shame on us. Stealing from Mother Church!' said the youth carrying his cloak. 'Is he coming after us?'

'I can't see,' said his friend, swinging the net over his shoulder now so that the carp leapt and thrashed in the small of his back. 'Let's get out of sight. Over here.' He peered over a dry stone wall, then, dropping the net over first, wriggled across it, his cloak catching in every crack and crevice.

'God preserve us, John, why do I go along with you?'

'Don't know, Musgrave,' said the other, slithering into a deep, short trench close to the wall amid a chute of gold, shimmery fish. 'Since you wouldn't lay a net to the water, I can't fathom it.'

Robin Musgrave joined John Exton in the trench, their four legs a confusion between them. 'You know I've a mortal dislike of water,' he said, grinning.

'God's Truth! It's only as deep as a man's chest. Take a man fishing and he sits five yards from the water!'

2

'I held my peace, didn't I?' Musgrave picked up one of the carp and it writhed gently. Its dark fins flickered against his hand, and the peculiar tusked mouth cursed him, the gill flaps opening and straining as if the fish were trying to lift off its head with each ineffectual twitch of its too-little fins. Even in the darkness of the ditch, he could see the colours wreathe into a fading rainbow of grey and gold, orange and white, blue and yellow.

'Have you ever seen the like?' Exton whispered, enthusiastically offering Musgrave another as long as his own forearm. 'And the taste! The Abbot sends them down to the castle, but there's no man beyond Barnard that's eaten one.' (The monks did not signify.)

'Mother Church in the vanguard of progress again,' said Musgrave dubiously. 'So how d'you know the taste's so good?' The dark earthen hole was beginning to take on that dank green smell of coarse fish. The carp in his hand gasped once more and died. 'What is this we're in?' He poked his head out of the trench.

'It's the grave dug for that woman hanged for abortioning. Two walls away from hallowed ground was the ruling, but she hasn't hanged out her time, I suppose.'

'Sweet Jesus.' Musgrave jumped to his feet, and the dead carp that had lodged in his lap tumbled down between his feet like a huge, colourless maggot. He kicked a foothole in the soil, stirrup high, and leapt out of the grave onto the open grass. From hands and knees he took off like a courser – over the stone wall, through the copse and downhill towards the town. John Exton followed, but, bundling together two cloaks and a fishing net, he fell far behind. He did not expect to catch up before they reached their own neighbouring gates but, between

3

the large oak and the start of the town, he saw Musgrave turn to face him, stumbling backwards a few steps with his own momentum, then falling out of sight off the bank and on to the stony street six feet below.

'Musgrave! You clown, Musgrave!' Exton shouted, running along the bank until he found a shallow way down. The girl at the bedroom window leaned out, alternating a laugh with an anxious shriek of 'Robin! Oh Robin!'

Musgrave was lying on his side, his face obliterated by dust, his arms in a circle round his head. As Exton reached him, he drew his knees up under his body but did not lift his head. His hands curled into fists, his neck, stretched from the edge of his collar into the gold of his beard, was strung with dark blue blood vessels, knotting and throbbing visibly under a powdering of dust.

'Musgrave, are you hurt?' said Exton, taking the head in his hands.

'Is he hurt? Is he all right?' called the girl from overhead.

'Musgrave, say something, for God's sake!'

But Musgrave could not speak: he rolled onto his back, clasping Exton's upper arm in an attempt to lift his head clear of the ground. His throat was scored by deep troughs where his windpipe dragged and sucked ineffectually. Exton waved the woman inside, but she took no notice.

'Robin, are you winded?' he asked.

Musgrave turned his face in to the crook of Exton's arm, shaking his head, and rolled on to his knees, rocking forward and back while a terrible whistling rattled through his chest.

'No, you're winded, Robin. Your sickness doesn't come on so fast.'

Musgrave knew that his fingers were tearing the sleeve out

4

of Exton's shirt – he could hear the seam rending beside his ear – but his spirit, swaddled in terror, had no power of movement. His body was hamstrung. There was no breath to stiffen his sinews. The sides of his boots scrabbled on the street. If he were to open his eyes, he knew he would be confronted with a gasping fish-head, flaring its gills and mouthing wordless obscenities an inch or two from his face.

Exton began to rub Musgrave's ribcage, supporting his head and running both hands from belt to collar. Musgrave sucked in a cry. Then the air cut a channel through his gullet, into his windpipe. After a minute or two he was able to sit up and begin to cough. Although his breath rattled like a stick dragged along a fence, he grinned at Exton and pulled himself to his feet.

'The excitement,' he said haltly. 'The prospect of eating those carp of yours. I was ... My breath went ahead of me. Let's take ourselves out of this place, can we, friend?' He hooked an arm round Exton's neck, reeling like a drunken man. 'Oh God, my ankle's broken, isn't it?'

'Musgrave, oh Musgrave!' Overhead, the girl Mary leaned over the sill, the ends of her shift's sleeves waving beyond her fingertips. 'I'll make it better. Let me make it better, Robin!' Her offer crescendoed to a wail, as Musgrave and Exton lurched three-legged up the hill. 'You'll come and visit me, won't you, Musgrave? Exton, tell him to come and see me! I was so afraid for you, Musgrave!'

Musgrave lifted a hand above his head and waved, without looking back.

Inwardly, he was nauseous and awash with melancholy. Surely the same distemper that blocked up the passages to his lungs settled itself afterwards in an impostume, for he needed to hide such a deal of misery when his attacks subsided. But

5

melancholy was not a humour to be indulged. So when finally Exton asked, 'What does the physician say?' Musgrave broke away from his support and began an impersonation:

'*You're finely bred, my boy. Delicately bred. Avoid inclemency! Forswear incontinency!* ... How many years has he been telling that to young men, do you think, to keep them indoors when he's abroad?'

'And what does he tell the girls, do you think?'

Musgrave looked over his shoulder furtively, then inclined his head towards Exton. 'Very much what I tell them, I think, given that we are both allowed the privacy of the bedroom.'

Exton pushed him away, renewing his support a moment later. 'But you take your surgery far and wide, friend. You hawk your cure-all round the entire province. Besides, they fall sick at the sight of you. Sick of love, or so they say.'

'No, no. Most of them just fall, and not for the first time. Anyway, who are you to defend the doctor's claims before mine? He's had his time. He's been through the fields taking the heads off the flowers, and a man ought to hand down his scythe to a younger fist when the time comes. Besides, John ... I whet my scythe more than I use it.'

Exton let the words fall between them. He was not certain whether he had been intended to hear the last. He would have liked to think that Musgrave feared his affliction; it certainly unnerved Exton. But the scattered clouds that drifted across Musgrave's relentless brightness were so slight, so unfixable, that Exton could never be sure whether there was substance to them or not.

'Is your ankle really broken?'

'Really? No. But it'll do for a reason to let go the hunt today. I shall exaggerate – if you'll second the story.'

6

'You don't want to go?'

Musgrave looked scornfully at Exton. 'What? An army of men abreast, storming through the forest while all the animals cower underground for fear of being outnumbered? Barnard telling his wartime anecdotes? Riding in such close convoy that Percival Fitzjohn's excitement is not to be contained for the brushing of knee against knee? Drinking at dry ditches and sleeping in wet ones? Rending God's rams out of thickets and slaughtering them as an alternative to slaughtering one another for boredom? A surfeit of al fresco joviality? Shall I tell you what I'll do, if I escape all that?' He sat down on the side of a public trough at the top of the street. A girl was watering her goat at it, her hair hanging forward in two clouts to her waist as she avoided looking at him. He watched her fixedly, waiting to catch her eye, but she turned away with eyes still lowered and, although her hair fanned out a little, he won hardly a sight of her face. 'I shall sleep till nine, eat a leisurely and civilised breakfast and stroll down to the church to see the ladies come out of mass. I shall flatter a girl too young to know I exaggerate, or flirt with a married woman old enough to know I'm joking.'

'Talk, talk, talk …'

'Ah, but you see that even my predictable, repetitive life is more than a match for a three-day hunt – the Lord Barnard's refined gift of torment.'

'Talk, talk. You don't know what it is to be in liege to a bad lord. Barnard's a good man.'

Musgrave snuffed up the air with profound pleasure. The sweet reek around the trough was mixed with the scent of acacia from the hill. He contemplated abusing Barnard for his strange, crow-like walk or snorting laugh, but it was something too close to blasphemy to overstep his station so far. And

7

besides, Barnard owned something too valuable to invite Musgrave's satire. He contented himself with saying, 'That doesn't make it a blessing to be invited to hunt with him. You know I don't like that sort of thing.'

Exton, tiring of flicking water out of the trough on to a black beetle in the road, started as he found Robin looking him in the eye.

'Comparing your swords and your scars and your rapes and wars, like women compare babies.'

When Musgrave spoke like this, with his top lip drawn back from his teeth, it seemed as though he was grinning. But Exton recoiled inwardly.

'Well! To run about killing things to prove you're alive,' Musgrave went on relentlessly. 'There's no art to it. The curtain of civilisation is easily rent nowadays, that's all, and behind it there's a heathen worship of the barbaric. Or so it seems to me.'

Exton's slowness in assimilating the long sentences only excited Musgrave more.

'Barnard's swords! You must have heard about Barnard's new Italian swords, yes? Two in one. A dubious device if he puts it on his coat of arms, I'd say. Two swords in one sheath ... Ach, my mind's infected. To see such pictures. But he talked about it like it was a symbol of manhood – as if he'd be glad of a war to put his swords to some use.'

Exton felt a familiar squeamishness. He would have liked to change the subject. He refused to ask what was wrong with war, so as to dam up one opportunity for Musgrave to be ...

'You think I'm effeminate' said Musgrave, reading his friend's face as plain as a letter, 'because I fall down and choke if I see a corpse and because I don't indulge in the manly pastimes of shooting sheep and abusing women.'

8

'Ah, so it's a joke, is it?' Exton laughed with relief. 'No woman's safe from you!'

'People believe I'm working my way through all the women in Christendom. I don't know why. It's mathematically unlikely, since I wait to be asked, that I've accomplished more than those who don't.'

'Don't what?'

'God damn you, Exton. You're not listening!' A great irritation plucked bodily at Musgrave. 'What's the use in talking to you? You're one of them.'

It was fiercely unjust. 'Me? Abuse women?'

'Admit it. They're a breed, they're a strain for you. They're like a fieldful of cattle – a crown a head, and indistinguishable. Isn't that right?'

'No! By the saints, it's not! And you know it isn't right! Word-mongerer. Have you forgotten who you're talking to?'

Musgrave's face crumpled. He covered it with his hands. 'Yes, yes. Yes, I had, man. Forgive me. 'Shrew me, man, I'm sorry. You love your Elizabeth. What a midden-mouth I am. God yes, Elizabeth.'

'And you. What do you know about love like that?' said Exton, still bridling.

'Domestic, hearth-rug love. Nothing. You have me right. Nothing at all.' He moved fast enough round the trough to catch Exton unawares and hug him close in both arms.

Exton bellowed in his ear, '*So what are you talking about?* Is there some woman for you, like Elizabeth for me?'

Musgrave knocked his forehead against Exton's collar bone, withdrew to arm's length, clapped his hands sharply against his friend's shoulders, and moved off down the street at a limping gallop. 'For me? What? A fieldful of flowers for picking, that's all. A fieldful of indistinguishable cattle! A fieldful of ... besides, what's the use in wanting the lily of the world when she's already stuck in another man's ... Eh? Isn't that right, you butcher of boars? You destroyer of deer! You router of rabbits! Who shall I seduce while you are away at the hunt? Eh?'

2

LORD BARNARD OPENED HIS EYES and watched three bedbugs, fat and red with blood, returning up his pillow towards their nest in the corner pillar of the bed. He wondered in what soft crease of his body they had spent the night. Crushing them one by one on the linen, he turned his head away from the stain, to savour his sweetest sight of the day: the Lady Barnard.

It was as if the rod of sunlight through the narrow window had struck the old bed like Moses striking the rock, and Elinor had sprung up to water his old age. She lay asleep beside him in her pool of hair, and her sleeping hand opened and closed near her mouth, as if she were drinking.

The Lord Barnard was still a few years away from being old: a full-fed, healthy man of forty-eight, with a disposition that kept his bloodstream wholesome and his liver largely free of bile. But he had an ageing image of himself, perhaps because his responsibilities weighed on him like so many years. They pressed like the bricks of an arch against the keystone, and he felt the mortar grind from time to time. But in Elinor was all the youth he needed in a morning. He picked up a hank of her hair, and it was as heavy as a horse's tail.

'What are you doing? What's the matter?' She came from the other side of sleep as if it were a waterfall, her mouth and eyes pursed tight.

'I'm sorry. I roused you.'

Her eyes opened; he saw the pupils contract as though he were falling from them and they diminishing with distance.

'Only you could rouse me, my love. You know that.' She arched her back under the bedclothes, and at the smell of her night's sleep all the little fledgling birds in his heart's nest opened their mouths and strained for the taste of her. The vow did nothing to change that.

But she slid from between his arms. When he stirred to follow her across the bed, he found that leaning on his elbow had creased the feeling from his arm. He toppled on to his face, and she laughed at him.

Yesterday's dress quickly covered the slit in the back of her smock where her skin had showed through as she slept. She was all grey wool and knotty laces in a moment, bending over beside the window and brushing her hair down into a harvest-coloured stook. The vow did nothing to diminish her beauty.

'How many people will be going on the hunt?' she asked.

'Oh fifteen, twenty. You had no need to rise this early,' said Lord Barnard, pulling on his clothes. 'You could have slept another hour or more.'

'I suppose old John Furleigh will be bringing along that witless son of his.'

'The boy keeps out of the way,' he said gently.

'Oh well. It's nothing to me. It won't be me who listens to his clicking and mooing. How weary you will be of male company when you return — if you can call some of them male. Will you wear your new swords? I'll strap them on for you.'

'Now Elinor. You know they're for armour. I explained to you ... You can fasten on this belt of mine. And tell me that your love for me is as it was yesterday.'

She threw back her hair: it was all air and sunlight, fluffed out like spun sugar. As she crossed the room and knelt down in front of him, his thickening body felt transfigured, by this woman on her knees, into some gilded iconic saint. It made her vow almost unforgiveable.

'How shall I make the hours pass until you come home to me?' she said, pulling the big belt prong through to the farthest hole her strength would allow. 'I'll be lonely and bored.'

As she moved to stand up again, he grasped her head between his hands and pressed it against his belly – so hard that, when he let go, an impress of the buckle was left on her cheek. Her breasts pressed against him: he could feel them against his wide thigh.

'God help me!' she cried, her voice muffled hot through his breeches. 'God arm me against temptation!' and she pulled away from him, crossing herself. 'Barnard! What's to become of me if you behave like that? Will you force me to break my vow?'

Barnard moved backwards, patting at the air as if to silence it.

'Because, if you are going to break my vow, I'd best spend your absence doing penance and mortifying myself!'

Still Barnard moved backwards, fending off the suggestion like a wasp. 'Forgive me, little wife. My Elinor. Don't distress yourself. Dearest woman. I'm a simple man. I can't understand this kind of delicate female foolishness.'

'Foolishness? My little effort at purity? You know I prayed to Saint Friedeswide and she made you look kindly on me. I might have promised her anything – anything – out of gratitude. Did I promise too much? Is a year too much? Did I? If I had the holiness of Saint Friedeswide I would have promised ...'

'Quiet, woman. That lady's name's a blight on me. It's my opinion that her husbands should have been raised to the ranks

13

of the blessed, not her. Lifelong virginity! Pah! Think on, woman. Think on till I come back.'

Angry more with his brutish mishandling of his wife than with her irritating sensibilities, Lord Barnard left the room. A moment or so later he returned, on the pretext of fetching his gloves, and allowed Elinor to cup his face between conciliatory hands and bestow the usual kisses on him: kisses which filled his spleen with the simmering liquor of his newly-married love. Her silly, fashionable vow was better, after all, than the alternative fashion of loose lasciviousness which besieged his small, secure nest. And if the good Lord spared him from the rigours of the hunt, perhaps the sappy spring that was entwining his castle keep with belladonna would thrust its sap into his little wife's blood, too.

Leaving on their left the pig-pen and on their right the dovecotes, Barnard's party of huntsmen passed the cook's meat-boy, standing with a dead swan dangling from a tailer. 'Tell the cook to serve my lady the tenderest parts in a stew of wine,' he called, and stirred his horse into a lumbering gallop.

The Lady Barnard turned away from the window and let the scarf she had been waving fall on to the priedieu. Then she stretched herself, as if she would push out the panels of the ceiling, and began unfastening the grey dress.

'Boy!' Her foot-page, a lad of about eighteen, came in from the corridor. He stood sagging at one knee nervously, so that his kneecaps crossed, or would have but for the great, loose fatness of his legs.

'Fetch me a bath. I'm going to church at nine.' His eyes loitered on her laces with their long tally of knots, and she rewarded the look by telling him to help her with a fastening.

As he did so, she ran her eyes over him appraisingly. 'What's your name again?'

'Geoffrey, lady.'

'Yes, of course. Geoffrey. Scrivenor's Geoffrey.'

'Yes, lady.'

'You're fat, Geoffrey.'

'Lady?'

'Grossly fat, Geoffrey. Even your fingers are fat. That will do now. Fetch the bath.'

Geoffrey fled, pursued to the head of the stairs by her laughter, and when the bath was standing in front of the tall stone mantelpiece, its steam making tiny sparkling drops on the goldwork of the bed's awning, Elinor almost shut the bedroom door, and laid aside the grey dress.

Outside in the corridor, Geoffrey – carrying yet another pitcher of hot water, and finding the door closed round, and bending in such a way as to set the water down, and glimpsing the flicker of movement inside the room – stayed for some time outside the room, enjoying a mixture of emotions.

He noticed how the snaky S of hair escaping down her neck darkened slightly with wetness. He noted how the vertebrae of her spine kept a longer tally than the knotted laces of the grey dress. He noted that the beads of sweat below her ears were more oval than the ones which burst through the palms of his own hands. He noted how soft little hairs on her skin formed a golden fichu between her shoulder-blades, and that her ribs were clearly visible from the base of the blades right along their curved journey towards . . .

'Fetch me the green dress, Geoffrey – the green velvet dress and the cream stomacher. And a laundered smock.'

He clattered against the ewer. He protested that he was not

15

there. He promised to put out his eyes if he had seen anything at all.

'The green velvet, Geoffrey,' she said, and he pushed the door and allowed himself an unimpeded view of paradise. 'Then you can take the dirty linen away.'

He stole her smock. But it was not missed among so many of the crisply tucked and ribboned white ones in the presses.

'WHERE'S THE LITTLE MUSGRAVE?' asked Elizabeth Fettimore, shielding her eyes against the low morning sun as Exton approached her house. She was sitting on a high stool in the front garden, spinning thread. The long bobbin that swung beside her skirts like a pendulum ticked away the moments in wobbling elipses. 'Won't he go with you on the hunt?'

'He's hurt.'

The bobbin nodded against a bed of rosemary, and her thread snagged among the long combs of soft green needles. Over-eagerly, Exton was on his knees freeing it.

'How early you rise, Liza. Is the whole of your household awake so early?'

'Thrift, master Exton,' she said with a slight frown hovering between her eyes. 'My father used to say that thrift with money is barely a virtue alongside the husbandry of minutes. How is he hurt?'

'I beg your pardon?'

'How badly has Robin hurt himself?'

'Oh. Just enough to keep him from going to the hunt. He's as idle as a pond, that one.'

'Nonsense, Exton. You do talk such nonsense.'

Exton was put out. He stood up and brushed his knees. He did not want to be talking about Robin Musgrave: there were few enough times when he spoke to Elizabeth without being in company. He had been trying, in any case, to put the early morning out of his mind.

'Not one of his fits?' she asked anxiously.

'Do you know of them, then? How many people know of them?'

She did not answer, but stood up to set the bobbin spinning again.

'I must be going,' he said, but sat down on the stool. 'How are your sisters?'

'God be thanked, they're well. My mother ...'

'Not ill, I hope?'

'No. God be praised.'

'God be praised,' he responded automatically.

'My mother says that they will be the death of him.'

'Who? What?'

'The fits.'

'What! The pox'll kill him first!'

Exton got up from the stool and plunged about the front garden, as though a diversion might stop her attributing the gross remark to him. He had come here in search of a sign from Elizabeth that he should approach her mother and her uncle. And here he was, with all the delicacy of a dray horse, trampling her mother's flowers and slighting his friend and giving offence.

'I must be gone now: the hunt's leaving,' he said, but he did not go.

Elizabeth had returned to her stool. Blood in the shape of small wings flushed each cheek, and she was biting her lip. 'Exton,' she said, in a low, emotional voice. 'If you came here with any purpose other than to annoy me, you had best go without speaking.'

'I wanted to say ...'

'I know it.'

'Oh!'

'And I have tried to intimate that I hold you a dear and good friend. And that my sentiments towards you are not less than a little tied to your gentle feelings for a mutual friend of ours.' She paused and then plunged on, her head hard down, like a curbed pony. 'And that while your friend Robin Musgrave breathes, my affections can turn only halfway towards any other man. You have no call to defame him to me: I know him for what he is, I think.'

And then she cried, and Exton, although he kicked a tuft of allyssum out of the base of the garden wall and looked at her for such a time that he became unaware of either time or tears — finally left the garden.

He snorted to himself as he led his horse down towards the midden and the urgent noise of Barnard's wolfhounds. He snorted aloud to infect himself with the humour of the situation, but could not. His horse looked at him with the same detached irony as the Little Musgrave. The women in the street looked at him as if each one was comparing him with the savour of Musgrave.

He whistled several times with amazement, but felt none. It made complete sense to him for Elizabeth to love Robin. Everyone did. Trolloping little maids and coarse, buxom, sailor's daughters, and the widows of sextons, and brown hop-pickers on middle-distant carts. And the girl in the upstairs room. And Liza Fettimore. And he, John Exton.

4

MUSGRAVE'S ANKLE WAS SWOLLEN and beginning to bruise when he arrived home. As he rounded the corner of his stable he could hear the drum of hooves and the rant of hounds, receding into the blue hollow of the valley.

He had been going to take his horse up on to the bluff, but decided against it. As he crossed the central yard, a strangely black and trailing creature stumbled across his path. A falcon, still wearing its hood and trailing its jesses, staggered drunkenly in a circle on the hard brown earth. Its hood so matched its colouring that it looked like something decapitated, lifting each foot rhythmically in after-death spasms. But it rolled up to Musgrave and managed a single jump, bending its bagged head towards its feet.

Its jesses had broken, he supposed, and it had wandered across the road from Exton's courtyard: it could hardly have come farther, blundering along blindfold on its large feet and short legs.

He fetched a glove, but only with a further bundle of cloth round his fist was he able to pick up the bird and carry it to the kitchens. He found it some rabbit meat and fed it — clumsy and gauche, since he owned no falcons himself. There was a fascination in the cleaver head bending and tearing. A man would have had to close his eyes to tear off such hunks of meat, but the falcon ate open-eyed, staring at the air, at Musgrave, at the meat-hook, at the window, all simultaneously, without preference. It held Musgrave's hand in its talons like a later course of food held in reserve.

He wrapped the broken ends of the jesses round his wrist and felt, for the first time, that umbilical link that infects falconers with the ferocity of their birds. He would go to the heath behind the church and see what the creature could do. If it was part-trained or refused to return to a strange glove, Exton's bird was no more lost than it had been before it stumbled into the courtyard.

He passed the church just as mass ended. The doors were opening and two priests, as black as crows, flapped past him and through the lychgate. He set the bird on a wall, headless again in its dark bag, and stayed to watch the ladies come down, as he had done many times before.

They fluttered out of the door like the small birds that must have multiplied during the forty-day captivity on the Ark: linnets and pigeons, doves and wrens and finches – their voices a high, tangled dissonance. The older women in brown and grey and black were drab by comparison with the girls in their courting plumage, slashed sleeves lined with flashes of red and blue and green.

Little Angela, the miller's daughter, was in her best white wool, plump and heavy like a fleece folded wool-side-in. Mistress Elizabeth and the other Fettimore sisters knew the virtue of pastel colours (as they knew every other virtue). La belle Katherine, who boasted she had been in France a week before, had on a peacock-coloured overdress and was chevroned with broad, blue, unflattering bands. And fat Anna had broken her laces between the shoulderblades. The merchant Belper's wife was in red velvet.

Not a braid or lace panel escaped Musgrave as he leaned against the churchyard wall. The concentrated smell of their perfumes and pomanders competed with the flowers, but he savoured their sweetness more with his eyes. Still there was one to come down: one at least. He would have continued on his way, but for that one face missing.

'Good morning, Robin,' said Elizabeth Fettimore, stepping off the path to address him. 'I heard that you were kept from hunting by a hurt.'

'My heart was dislocated from the thought of mangling civilised creatures in the company of savage people,' he replied, defensive, as he always felt with the oldest Fettimore girl.

'And yet, you're planning to spend the morning hawking? It was the company that most deterred you, then, and not the practice.'

'Will you blame me for preferring the present company?'

'Oh yes, Robin. While your refinement cannot restrain you from eating off all the plates on the table.'

'Oh, but God laid the table with such care, Liza! How can I resist such a feast?' She seemed to wilt a little. 'Pay no attention to me. It's not true. I'm not as good a man as John Exton, but I know my faults better than he does. You shouldn't believe everything he says about me.'

'Do you suppose your friends discuss you in private, Robin?'

He was discomposed by the blush, and said hastily, 'Of course, there are more important subjects between lovers. Forgive me.'

A flurry of white issued from the church door like doves from a cote. But it was a nun's surplice billowing out with the wind. There was *surely* another face to come. Or perhaps it had not been there today, among the other faces.

'John Exton is not my lover, Robin,' said Elizabeth Fettimore in her soft, prayerful voice.

There, then on the steps. Not linnet or dove-coloured, but there, in olive-green velvet, slashed sparingly with red silk, as though some thin beak had slashed its way into that dense plumage. Her face was unquoifed, but with a square of white silk over her hair, her plaits half-unbraided. There was so much sheen to her – hair, velvet, silk, skin – that she glistened like water. And he, Tantalus, in his lake of fiery passion, burned out of reach of her.

Elizabeth looked over her shoulder to where his eyes reached out, drowningly. 'John Exton is not my lover,' she repeated as she linked her hands low down in front of her, and stepped back on to the churchyard path.

'Good-day, Mistress Fettimore,' he said absently, and behind his back the stonewalling shifted and grated, stone against stone, as he pressed his shoulderblades against its flints.

The falcon drew himself up and spread its wings until the longest feathers touched above its hood, then it snapped shut into a huddled, stump on the wall, and only its claws continued, grating yellow spoors off the stone.

Robin Musgrave went on burning in his parochial pond of fire, and bent his adoration towards the church, as the Diocletian martyrs must have done who burned within sight of Rome.

Her sweetness was ambrosial: a thing of myth and rumour. He held it his most sure and certain belief that, resting his eyes on her, he could suffer death by inches and be unaware of it. Night nor old age, nor fire nor wa … earth could envelop him, but his soul would cling safe to the rails of radiance that hinged on this woman.

The rocks of the wall grated behind him, and the black

yew beside the church pointed its black, flame-shaped shadow towards him as the morning sun pulled its full circle over the church roof.

This was the morsel of flesh he had kept from any mouth. Even John Exton, who was his closest friend and a man of integrity, was not to be trusted with the mention of this woman. He and all the other men Robin knew held women in their conversation like the troll holds its victims – until the hot blood and grease trickled down their jaws. But he, Robin, had withheld this one delicacy.

'I am a man of unclean lips and I dwell in the midst of a people of unclean lips.' The words crept unforgiving into his thoughts.

But he carried this lady where the travelling priest carries the holy wafer in a pyx, somewhere under his robes and over his heart. The pillar of her light sustained him across a wilderness of loneliness. A blessing from her could redeem him from the Outer Darkness. Her purity blotted him out as he wished to be blotted out.

The other women would mince and simper and signal him, and he would click his tongue at them, flatter them or follow them, desultory, up the earth path, half the way home to their husbands. Pollute, profane, prey on, please them – placate them. But this lady would stay, as the madonna would stay in her chilly niche after the sweaty congregation and their acrid prayers had vacated the church. She remained a permanent; immoveable, undefilable mystery, without gilt, without guilt.

Musgrave was sweating. He felt the sweat creep down his temples and his palms, although there was a cold edge to the wind. He turned to escape the strength of his feelings, and tried to pick up the falcon. But the creature, swamped in agitated, distressful scents, struggled against the jesses and fouled his

24

glove. He threw the animal down in disgust, into the well of the wall where it rocked ridiculously, bending its no-head down and then stretching upwards in pursuit of its dignity.

Steps moved towards him along the church path. If he were to turn ... Exton was right to suggest he was womanish. He was afraid of his own bloodstream, beating its plundering way uphill. He envied the other men their barbarous, mercantile attitude to women. He envied them their freedom from the pain of this woman approaching him.

'You're Robin Musgrave,' she said, blotting out his iniquities in the dark shadow she cast ahead of her.

'Lady.'

'I hear your name mentioned.'

'We are related. Your husband's uncle's ...'

'Ah yes. But I've heard your name more often from the ladies of my acquaintance, God gave you a good face, Musgrave.'

'God was mistaken when He ...' An idea had formed itself in Musgrave's head but went astray before he could speak it.

'Mistaken? They say Lucifer was beautiful. Are you Lucifer, then?'

'No, lady.' (He groped for coherence.) 'Or how would I be in the company of angels now?'

She could feel him burning. He knew it, for he could see the scorch colouring her skin as it would if she was beside a bonfire.

'You are sweating, Robin.'

He dried his hairline with the heel of his bare hand, apologising. 'Pain's always next to beauty, madam.' His Christian name was still clamouring inside his head where her use of it had set it swinging like a cacophony of bells.

'Is that so? Let me tell you a secret, Robin Musgrave.' She gave him her handkerchief, bending forward from the waist to

25

press it into his hand. 'I'm exceedingly hot myself.'

The church's windvane creaked round to point north: the wind was icy. Exton's falcon, in the dip of the wall, cocked its lack-of-head towards the sound — one bird acknowledging another. Robin kissed the handkerchief in an onrush of sentiment, and would have pressed it back into Lady Barnard's hand if he had not noticed it pick up some of the yellow gel from the back of his wrappered glove.

5

'YOU SAID HE WAS ALWAYS TALKING. He didn't talk at all.'

'You took him by surpise, I daresay, madam,' said Joan, as she removed her mistress's over-sleeves. 'I don't like this dress, lady. Green's for fairies and jewesses. It's bad luck for Christian folk.'

'And he scarcely even looked at me,' said the Lady Barnard. 'He spoke more to Elizabeth Fettimore than he spoke to me.'

'Who dressed you this mor'n, and me so late, with my boy took bad, lady?'

'I dressed myself, of course. Don't take all day, Joan.'

'Patience, madam, patience. You're all knots.'

They stood in front of the fire in the big dining hall. The house rattled, empty of servants and callers, so many had gone on the hunt.

'Dirty Mary says he's like Cain and Abel both together, between the sheets,' said Elinor.

'I don't doubt but Dirty Mary's had nothing to do with the fellow. No mor'n she's got sheets. He's not one to be eating off a canker tree. He knows what's good for'm — and he's far too sickly, besides.'

'Well, he hardly spoke to me, that's all.' She watched Joan picking at the knot between sleeve and bodice, as a horse vacantly watches its groom. It was hard to believe that Joan

27

had a young son: she was raddled. 'I think I look well enough in green.'

The older woman's face – a yellow, tallowy consistency – crazed and crinkled into a grin. 'Well he thought well enough of it, that's certain. Or the lady inside it.' Her voice was as crackled as her skin, but when she laughed there was a strange self-assurance to it, like the singing voice of someone who knows they have perfect pitch.

Elinor, who had been waiting for the smallest encouragement, giggled with satisfaction. 'He did seem ... excitable. He did *breathe* so.'

'And he has your scarf still, madam.'

'Yes, he has. He has.' She did not consider herself to be confiding in her serving-woman. Joan was simply a source of confirmation for her thoughts: anything less than accord could simply be disregarded, for the woman was only a gipsy, after all. 'He's so very beautiful.'

A long silence was allowed to settle over the words. It settled like a canopy over the thought of Musgrave, and under the canopy, the full panoply of a woman's imagination settled on Musgrave's shoulders. How could anything so lovely to look at not be a thing to desire?

All her life she had learned that the beautiful was to be aspired to: the material, so as to be fashionable; the decking of the madonna, so as to be devout; the jewelled throat and hand, so as to maintain a man's prestige. Barnard was ugly – unbeautiful, at least. And ugliness was a thing to be put out of mind – like the Plague, like the darkness, like the works of the Devil (whatever they were).

'I must have him, Joan. I must have him before Barnard comes home. You fetch him here. I love him. Dirty Mary says ...'

'I've heard different about this one,' Joan said, moving nearer to the table where breakfast stood awaiting the return from mass, She dared not pick at it first, but she could scrag a handful of meat as soon as Elinor had plucked holes in the joints. 'There's a saying among the People ...'

'Oh be quiet, you old witch.'

'There's a saying, *A man's not a man less a maid's a mother.* I don't hear tell of any babes hereabouts with the Little Musgrave's prettiness. And people do say he's got a falling sickness. He may talk. But there's a saying, *Words prove nought but the size of a man's tongue.*'

'Any more of your gipsy sayings and I'll hang you myself, you old crab. Go and find my Robin and tell him ... Say ...'

'What, lady?'

'Tell him ... he's won my heart altogether out of me ...'

Joan blew her nose into her hand with a noisy scepticism.

'No. No. First find him and say ... ask him ...'

'What, madam?'

'Ask him what he would do ... what he would give to sleep with the Lady Barnard. And bring me word what he says. Go now. Go right away.'

No breakfast. Joan pulled away regretfully from the table. 'I'll go. But he'll maybe not come.'

At seventeen, Elinor Barnard had a few of the arts of womanhood still to master. But none of the sharp implements of absolute authority escaped her in the handling of castle servants. 'Gipsy woman, I'll tell you what. No meat or drink for you until the Little Musgrave's in my lap. I'll send Geoffrey with you to hold you to your word.' She searched a moment for the absolute refinements of the threat. 'And if you breathe one word to him of what you're about, or if he tells me you break your bargain,

I'll hand you over to the gipsy-hunters in time for the next hanging. Geoffrey!'

Geoffrey sat in the window-slitted service garret which overhung the grassy foundation mound like a ship's after-cabin overhanging the wake. A keen wind lifted the lower limbs of the sheepskin hung over the end window, so that from time to time it beckoned him.

But he would not stir from the stool where he sat, hands clasped between his knees, immersed in imagination. There were days when his imagination served him for passage all the way out of the service hall, clear out of the biting wind which lifted the skin flap and eddied like cold water between the beds. On such days he clutched his imagination to him and crept out of sight, into some corner, and sat very still so as not to jolt the visions out of his brain. They were as brightly coloured as any mystery play. There, rough and ready people were entitled to gorgeous costumes and a high dais. Ordinary working men enjoyed a fluent, uninterrupted chance to speak. A common man, by common consent, could aspire even to acting God ...

Inside Geoffrey's imagination, all the disadvantages hamstringing a timid servant boy – a youth weltering inside bloated obesity, with thinning hair and weak wrists – inside his imagination, all those accidents of birth were lifted. He doubted whether any other person – even one with Latin or a waist – was capable of raising the visions he could conjure, if he was left in peace. The pageant-cart, the cast, the script of the play all fell under his direction. And there he sat, on a gantry of self-esteem, as beautiful as the archangel Michael, as articulate as the Devil, as desirable as sin.

The incident of the bath had made damaging inroads on

his walled imagination. For an hour or more, his composure shattered, real images and recollections teemed through the breach and quite overpowered his well-rehearsed imaginings. It was almost routine now, the daydream sequence in which he, Geoffrey, was knighted in the selfsame battle which lamentably felled the Lord Barnard, and he, Geoffrey, being the one to bring the sad news to the Lady Elinor, comforted her as a prelude to him, Geoffrey, wooing her. Beside the reality of his liege lady's nakedness, such sequences dried up and blew away.

But sitting perfectly still, his hands clasped between his knees, he was beginning to struggle back into the familiar castle of his brain. Dragging behind him his trophy of great worth, he patched up the breached walls, drove off the cold reality that beckoned him from the end window, and prepared for a new, ambitious sequence.

Was it not conceivable that a woman with such eyes might see into the heart of a man? And seeing the love there, might not a woman of her gentleness and charity pity him? And given the closeness of pity to love, might she not in time find herself loving him? And given her modesty and powerlessness to declare such a love, might she not chance one desperate signal, one wordless sign, one pure white flag brandished at him as he stood in her doorway? Might she not want him to return a sign and once, perhaps once, clothe their mutual passion in flesh?

Flesh. His great belly rested in his cupped hands and shook with emotion and the cold. The early morning sun had quite gone, and a miserable greyness besieged Barnard's fortified manorhouse. But, in its service garret, overhanging the foundation mound, Geoffrey Scrivenor triumphed inside his fortified brain. Only chastity and the peevishness of impotent clergy divided him from his mistress. And what a world of difference

31

now, when he called the lady his mistress!

'Geoffrey!'

'Yes, madam?' He hurried into the room, his heavy thighs slapping one another, his lungs labouring under the stress of hurrying down the steeply lashed steps from the garret. His eyes and mouth were wide, like a swimmer who has just surfaced from a long spell underwater ...

'Geoffrey. Come here,' said his mistress, smiling so sweetly, with her head so slightly inclined. He stepped closer. His amazement did not waver. She took his forearm between her hands and chafed it gently while she spoke.

'This old whore', she said, nodding towards Joan, 'is a gipsy.'

(Should he say that he knew it? That everybody knew it?)

'I've promised not to have her hanged if she does one small task for me,' said Elinor. 'On condition that she doesn't eat nor drink till it's done. I want you to go with her and keep her to her word. Will you do that for me?' And she slid her grip down to his fat white hand.

'Good.' And to Joan she said, 'Look to it, Joan. You'll not find a better guard dog than Geoffrey. He's my very own creature.'

6

Intermittently, the sun shattered the banks of cloud on the greenly tinged sky, like a stone dispelling the algae in a pond. Then the roof of the heath seemed so flat and bright that Musgrave almost expected to see his reflection flexing enormous above him. But afterwards, an easterly wind would stir up an opaque sediment, and weedy clouds would spread out again and intermingle.

He set the falcon down on a tree which had been wasted by lightning, and sat down with his back to the stump. He had not been to sleep all night, roaming about with Exton and the girls from the inn. He began to feel the need to close his eyes. But when he did so, the Lady Elinor's face burned on the ball of his eye and he woke up flinching.

She was more beautiful than breath to the dead. He thought that his joy in all womankind had been painlessly ruined by seeing Elinor. No one would ever compare with her.

The falcon's bells jangled in his ear. Too far off to recognise, a strange pair – mother and son? – dawdled out of the town in his direction. Foreshortening made their progress almost imperceptible. Across the valley it was raining into the forest, the cloud bases all ragged and torn on the treetops. John and Percival and the Lord Barnard and the rest would be running the gauntlet between the dripping tree branches that drove water through a man's clothes to his skin. Over Musgrave's dreamy exultation, the sky dared not even rain.

He had made a lure out of a chicken's wing on a rein, and had brought the remaining haunch of rabbit with him. But he held out little hope of the bird returning to him once he loosed it. It was not his. It was like Elinor, whose life was disjointed from his, with whom he had no link, no connection.

As he removed the hood and saw the great yellow eyes, fear ran him through momentarily: his cheek, his soft lips, his shallow-socketed, vulnerable eyes confronted the hook of the beak. Then the bird lifted off his wrist with a great downward thrust on the glove and one of the big wings brushed against his beard.

The tiercel spiralled and stood, spiralled and stood, as though it were climbing the stairs of some airy tower, pausing at each landing to view the window of sky. Then it jagged wildly from one cloud base to the next and over the treetops. Round the sky it swooped, like a mote on Musgrave's eyeball as he tried to follow it. Once or twice it sliced the blue-green sector of sky directly over his head, eyeing perhaps him, perhaps the rabbit carcase. Or perhaps the entire valley was condensed into the convex yellow iris. A pigeon murmured an uneasy murmur in the copse. A rook slouched across the far end of the sky. But the hawk saw a field mouse clinging like a tare to the stem of a wild oat and stooped on that.

The little creature was thrown into the air where both talons seized it forward of the beak. In turning his eyes away, Musgrave met the grin of an old woman. At second sight the face was not old, but slightly shrivelled and one that he knew as a reputed gipsy in service at the castle. Behind her, a fat pallid boy stood a few yards off, slouched on one bulging hip, inclining an ear as if he had been told not to listen.

34

'Do you have business with me?' Musgrave asked the woman.

'My lady's business,' said Joan. 'Farther off, Geoffrey!'

Robin put one hand to his doublet where the scarf was stuffed out of sight, and wondered if he could refuse its return.

'I'm privileged to have been in her thoughts since we spoke.'

'Sir, you've scarce been out of 'em.' She moved in close to him and took his elbow in both hands to draw him farther off from Geoffrey's craning. 'Your name's knowed at the castle, sir.'

'I'm related to your mistress. Distantly.'

'Not too close, I hope.'

'Distantly. I said, distantly.' A clammy sensation attached to Joan; he would have been glad to be rid of her hands on his arm, but her grip was tight.

'They clep you Little Musgrave,' she said, leering into his ear as he turned his head away from her breath. 'Why's that, sir? I hope you don't merit no such name.'

He scowled at her but her presumption was too astonishing for him to shake her off. And besides, she had her lady's words behind her black teeth. 'I hear quite another story from the maids here'bouts. Have you got such a thing as an apple about you, sir?'

'What?'

'No. No. But a woman deserves better treatment on business like this.'

'What business, woman?'

For all her impertinence, the gipsy seemed to find difficulty in phrasing her commission. Finally she lunged into it. 'My lady commands you visit her privily. With the huntsmen gone, she fears to be greatly lonely and much unthought of.' (She paused to savour the tremor which clenched Musgrave's muscles.) 'And you being a kinsman ... And you being so gentle born ...'

'While I'm living, madam, your mistress will not be unthought of,' he said.

Joan swelled with pleasure at the civility 'madam'. 'And you being so fair-faced, truly. She *is* a pretty little thing, isn't she though?' He shook her off, not hearing her for the pulse beating on his eardrums. But when she raised her voice for Geoffrey's benefit, he did hear her. 'You may call to see the Lordship's new purchase of Italian swords, sir,' she said, brushing her hips stiffly, conclusively. 'Milady does so love an expert swordsman.'

'I know nothing of swords, madam, but ... '

'I know, I know,' she whispered, nodding a warning towards Geoffrey, 'but you're well acquainted with the sheaths. Well, you come and quick sharp too, lording. Don't you keep my lady waiting or I'll be the one to suffer for it, I know. Shift your fat carcase, Geoffrey. Let's be moving closer to a table, you tallow dropping.' They set off – a halt pair – towards the town. One of them was hungry: Robin could hear the gurgle of stomach juices when they were both already labouring downhill.

With the stringy elastic of the mouse stretched between talon and beak, the tiercel watched Musgrave swing his hopeful chicken wing. Scornful of him, it finished its meal, then flew off, clinging close to the ground, tracing the mounds and hollows before taking a trajectory from the curve of an embankment and soaring upwards again. It flew into the white patch of sun which swallowed it.

Musgrave unshielded his eyes and brought his hands to rest on his head, spinning himself, instead of the lure, round and round in a whirling childishness. The falcon's talons clawed his bowels up and trailed them through the sky. The beating wings, even when they were out of sight, seemed to fill the air with their freedom. In staring after it into the sun, the patch of

36

white seemed to spread into the shape of a seraph with a superabundance of wings and, centrally, the face of Elinor, the Lady Barnard.

The giddy, whirling ground banked suddenly and hit him in the back but as he lay looking up at the sky, the archangel did not fade but bore down on him as though he were Isaiah in the smoking temple. His pure unreachable love was stooping on him with coals of fire clenched in her forked pinions. He allowed his body to roll down the incline of turf before letting the sky pour in at his eyes again. The seraph Elinor hung vastly over him, brandishing a particle of sun.

'I am a man of unclean lips, and I dwell in the midst of a people of unclean ... ' and he laid himself open on the ground to the tongs she brandished.

But as the sun forged its way out of cloud cover and its rays fell on to the heath, they swept first across Musgrave's legs. The seraph, with wings which blotted out all heaven, thrust the coals not on to his lips, as in the Bible story, but into his groin.

7

'SUCH A SIMPLETON!' bellowed Lord Barnard so loudly that a horse started and stumbled in its hobbles. 'If you want this woman, have her lad! Ask her? You've got no business asking her. It's nobody's business but yours and her father's.'

Barnard was butchering a wild pig for a roast, emphasising each of his words with rasping noises from the knife as it sawed through the hair and skin. The inside of the throat steamed in the rain. Both Barnard and Exton were wet through. The entire hunting party stood around Barnard and his pig like a wet paling fence, the dogs struggling and barking between them.

'Her father's dead, sir, these five years.'

'Well, her uncle, then. Christ, I'll make it my business to see you get the wench!'

Exton wondered how the subject of Elizabeth had reached Barnard at all, when it had begun as a casual remark to a man at the tail of the troop. And he wondered why he was not overjoyed at the thought of Barnard intervening. 'I'll do as you say, sir, but I was not looking for your influence.'

'Wish you joy, lad. Hold the snout, eh? Get a firm grip.'

Exton squatted down at the head of the female and took hold of the glassy-eyed head by an ear and the lower jaw, while Barnard lifted the back legs. They angled her for the spit. The pig would roast while they went on hunting (if a fire could be got going). Such an early kill was a consolation to the men, standing around in their heavily sodden clothes, watching rain spatter into their pig and the offal spatter out of her. Oswald brought the spit rod off the pack horse. Often, none of the roasting gear was used, when nothing offered itself up for killing. But then Lem came with the cold meat and drove back the barbarously dark green of the forest, and carved a civilised space out of its vicious brutish desolation. Barnard carried him with an aura of hearth and heat and home. His liege men lacked nothing. Even Exton if he wanted a wife, a specific wife, would be given the wife he wanted. Barnard was a good man to be with in the wet, obscure forest.

There was foolery over the spit. Furleigh and Edmund took it out of Oswald's hands and wrestled over it. An entertainment – Edmund always the clown. The men standing around cheered: the rainy woods hissed.

'Takes a man to handle one as long as this. Give it to me.'

'Mind the pig don't see you coming!'

'They all lie still for me!'

'Only if they're dead as pork ... '

'Or cold as mutton!'

'Let'm practice, lads. He don't get the chance too often.'

'Give'm room. Target's not generally so small.'

'It's Fitzsimmon needs the practice. We'll save the boar for'm.'

' ... save the boar for Fitzsimmon ... ' The forest gaped and swallowed their shouting.

' ... boar for Fitzsimmon ... '

'What are you waiting for, Edmund? Press home, boy. Pig's died of boredom.'

'Look on, Exton, you might learn a thing or two.'

In the scuffling and guffawing, Furleigh was hit a blow with the spit and sat on his heels clutching his head. Fitzsimmon had a boot pulled off and was looking for it in a leaf-filled trench.

Barnard, in laughing, had dropped the pig. From between Exton's hands its head looked up at him – reproaching their juvenile sense of humour. Men are men in the forest, he told its red-rimmed nostrils. But he suddenly envisaged Musgrave's picture of the little animals of the forest 'cowering underground for fear of being outnumbered'.

'Look on, Exton,' said the Lord Barnard. 'You may learn a thing or two about winning Elizabeth Fettimore.'

The spit penetrated the sow at the anus and their exertions at the rear pushed its head hard into Exton's lap.

'I wanted to marry with some ... a little ... chivalry,' he panted. 'Yes, ... chivalry. Your marriage to Lady Elinor – something chivalric, don't you agree, my lord?'

Barnard squatted by the pig's inverted haunch, his eyes rivetted on the slow, twisting entry of the metal into the crunching body cavity.

'You're out of your station, John Exton,' he said finally, frowning at the haunch. 'You think out of your station, boy. Concern yourself with bedding Mistress Fettimore and leave chivalry to your betters.'

Exton too watched the boring of the sow and wondered why he was not exultant with the same savage joy these men were feeling. Perhaps he had been poisoned (he told himself) by association with Musgrave's effeminate squeamishness.

'What message did she send him, Joan?' Geoffrey asked as she organised him into lifting her down on to the roadway. They walked close together on the way back, Joan cheerfully sociable at the thought of a job well done.

'Don't you trouble yourself over that, young lad. Ah, he's a pretty little thing, that Musgrave. Good thighs. Pretty manners.'

'He's a clown like his father,' said Geoffrey, habitually dismissive. 'D'you know, his father fell head first into a well and drowned. What a clown. And he's just a capon. The cook's wife says he's just a capon.'

Joan cackled raucously. 'You're as simple as she is.' She suspected that Geoffrey had no idea what the cook's wife meant by it and she was sure he lacked the imagination to read the jealousy in such a remark. She breathed a small, happy sigh at the thought of Lady Elinor having her way.

'I'm right fond of that lady wench, you know,' she said, and in saying so it became true. Joan's affections were founded in the present. Loyalty, since that relied on memories of past kindnesses, could not have taken root in her: for one thing there had been too few kindnesses – for another, her thoughts bowed to the mood of the moment. 'You're a pleasant enough boy, your own self, Geoffrey.'

He smiled and fell into step with her, though his mind was really on Elinor and the shift of hers that lay hidden under his palliasse.

'She kept you from the hangman, didn't she?' he said.

'When my Peder got took.' She remembered the day, although lapsed time had divorced her from the pain of it. 'They collared him to the lip of the master's drawbridge and raised it up.'

'I remember.'

'Could 'ear his feet drumming on the wood right from milady's bedroom. Hours after.'

'There was wind.'

'Yes. Yes, they do say t'was the wind. He had big feet, my Peder.'

41

They walked on in silence for a while, past the linnet breaks between the two hills. Linnets and blackbirds and wrens were suspended in mid-air, the nets invisible from the roadway, some still fluttering. They looked like moths on the outside of a tent against a strong moon. Now and then one would break free and fly off or fall to the ground. Somebody's valuable tiercel falcon had got itself snared — stooping probably on a bird struggling in the nets. It hung upside down by its big feet, its wide wings fanned open so that the tips met over its head.

'I was doing business with the Lady Elinor, I remember. 'Twas the week after the wedding and she'd a mind to have her future looked into. Somehow she heard we was passing through. They came and said to her what was a-doing outside ... 'Twas a bad summer for the People that last one. And I had Jacky with me. And that lady she had us both sit down on the priedieux and wait till the mob had gone off home. Hours, and Peder with his feet banging the while. Bless her for a good kind woman. By the window, they was, those priedieux. Know 'em?'

Geoffrey recollected the room. How much he remembered of things not knowingly looked at! 'How would I know, noodlehead? Have I been there?'

She dug him in the ribs with her elbow and laughed that witch-like cackle. 'You never know. Start small, work up to big.'

Joan might have to be put out of the way, thought Geoffrey. There was too much of the gipsy wisdom in her. Perhaps she could truly read a person's future. 'Did you look into Lady Barnard's future before they hanged your man?' he asked.

'Bless you, boy, yes. An' 'twas full of love. Brimful of love!'

They exchanged smiles of such mutual joy for their mistress's happiness that they could have walked two abreast into Heaven on the strength of them. He took her arm and handed her an

42

apple from the tail of a cart crossing into the market area.

'Not that I told her 'bout the blondness – being as Barnard's so dark and her fresh married to'm 'n all.'

'Blond? A blond man?' Geoffrey's hand lifted involuntarily to the nape of his neck where the strands were thickest of his pale, limp, Saxonish hair.

'Blond as any Musgrave, bless her. Oh I wish 'er such loving, boy, my own shanks shake for'r, don't your'n? That's what young folk be for, and don't you believe what any of them shrunk-up priests tell you. Bodies are made for doing and dancing and dandling, and I wish'r all the dances and doings she can win with the Little Musgrave fore'n Barnard gets her with child. And so do she.'

Geoffrey looked down at her arm under his, as if he had picked up a child and discovered it was a dwarf – a hideous, malformed hobgoblin that clung on with little burning claws and offered to melt down the sun and the moon to pay for a night or two in Gomorrah.

8

ELINOR COULD SEE HIM COMING, all the way from the linnet breaks to the corner of the market. Joan and Geoffrey had been well ahead: they were long since hidden by the row of houses at the back of the market place. She expected them to report to her at any moment. He would be much longer in coming. His steps were so slow: his paces were so short. It seemed as if he were walking in one spot and never came any closer.

But that was just as well. Now that he had her thoughts in his head, he frightened her. It was as if he could walk directly out of the streets and into her brain. She made herself vulnerable. But how vulnerable could she be to such a man when he looked so fragile among the turgid brown stones and heavy-fisted trees? He was like a glass vessel holding some alchemical mixture that would turn her to gold, pure gold. His hair glistened as it moved, like the sand in an hour-glass ... She had not set her heart so much on a thing since childhood.

She went to the door and looked for Joan and Geoffrey but they were not outside. Somewhere, a long way off, voices were squabbling which could have been theirs, but in the meantime Musgrave came nearer and nearer. She was loath to encounter him without being told his reaction – how his ardour had overflowed, how he had leapt for joy, how he had been lost for words at the honour of ...

The voices were recognisable now as Joan and Geoffrey,

screaming abuse at one another in the downstairs lobby. The sound of fright in their voices infected her: she ran to the door and thought that the sound of her feet on the stairs had silenced them. They were nowhere to be seen when she reached the hall: only Musgrave.

'Madam, forgive me,' said Musgrave, retreating beyond the draught curtain that hung across the room. 'I'm unannounced. Your servants seemed to take fright at the sight of me.'

'Surely not.' Her slippers skidded on the stone slabs as she broke her run. 'Oh, surely not.'

Musgrave ran one hand through his hair. It fell back, strand by strand, for some seconds. It was darker at the base: the summer bleaching of it had not yet grown out. Strand by strand, it fell back on to the curve of his skull.

'Sweet Jesus come to my aid,' thought Musgrave. 'She wants me.'

'You came very quickly,' she said, straightening her plaits over her breasts and straightening her spine inside the green dress.

'Before my time, perhaps. I shall go and return later . . . '

'No!'

He halted his backward creep beyond the curtain, reluctant to stay and be proved right, reluctant to go with such a mind full of squalor.

'What did Joan say to you?' she asked, her voice squeezed up an octave in her throat.

'She conveyed your generous invitation, lady. To view the Lord Barnard's new Italian swords. A pair, so I hear.'

'A perfect pair,' she breathed. She was dazzled by him: he scorched her retina. Consequently she saw only a blurred picture of him – a blurred agitation, and a flush on his cheeks. She

45

supplied the ardour out of her own fire and taking him by the wrist drew him towards the press in one corner of the room. 'Come here, Little Musgrave. Come and show me what you know about swordplay.'

'Nothing at all, madam. I know nothing about swords.'

'And play?' She opened the chest, took out a flat wallet of cloth, and unwrapped the swords. The twin scabbards each held a rapier, the simple oval handle of the shorter finishing at the rim of the longer sheath. The longer weapon had a far more ornate handle to it: a filigree guard worked with the interlacing of fantastic birds. 'I think they're cuckoos,' she said, resting her hand over his as he took hold of the decorated hilt. 'If it's Barnard's, they must be cuckoos. Do you like my husband, cousin?'

'He's my liege-lord, madam. God forbid I should do anything but love him in fealty!'

'God forbids everything,' she said poutingly, breaking from the corner of the room. 'God's old. He's an old man with old, cold blood in him, isn't he? He's like Barnard ... What else did Joan say to you?'

'Nothing, madam.' As he walked out into the middle of the room, she came and took the swords from him and drew one. She was all salt, thought Musgrave. Her arm was white as salt. Her throat and face were saltpetre white. He saw her with the eyes of Lot, and she had turned into a pillar of salt, her salt eyes bent fixedly on Sodom while his had been on lands of milk and honey.

'Have you ever been to Italy, Robin?'

'No, ma'am. My father went when I was only a child. He went. My father.'

She placed the point of the shortsword against her abdomen.

46

'Is it true that they disembowelled the Count of Bregazza with a sword in his own market place?'

'I have absolutely no idea, madam. Did you know the gentleman?' She reached out, took his hand, pressed the sword hilt into it and leaned forward on to the tip, her cheek almost touching his as she whispered, 'What would you give this day, Musgrave, to lie one night with me?'

He fixed his eyes, over her shoulder, on the rim of the fireplace. 'I would have given my estate to the man who had prevented me coming here today, madam.'

'Robin!'

How, if she was salt, he thought, could she drop through such shades of whiteness to this new pallor. Sheer charity made him want to say something to save her face, for loss of face seemed to take on physical shape with Elinor. This greatly chronicled beauty was as plain as Salisbury without the colour to contour her features. 'Madam,' he said without knowing what words would follow. 'Lady Elinor. If I had confided my secret to so much as a mute swan I could have understood its broadcast reaching you. Perhaps, like the Saviour among his crowds you felt my passion through the hem of your robe ... ' A shade paler still. 'I have loved you this long year past, lady. But the Lord God knows me for an arrant coward and I never thought to gratify my longing at the expense of my soul or your honour. I must ... continue to ... worship you as a non-communicant — excommunicated from the flesh and blood but not, I trust, from the spirit of my sweetest cousin ... ' What nonsense was this? The words fell out of him like sweat.

'I didn't understand that,' said Elinor, frowning, but she had understood a gist, a tenor which she liked, and one or two words she had understood since before they were said. 'So you love me, do you? Well, you need not be so unambitious, Robin. That's what I have been saying to you. You shall lie with me. Today, Robin. Now.'

He threw up arguments like a barricade on which she advanced with the longsword clapping in its double scabbard.

'I dare not, lady! Pray don't lay me bare to my cowardice! I dare not for my life, lady. I'm in fealty to your husband. What would become of me, lady, if I brought down on myself the might of his anger?' His gallantry pursued him like the unicorn through the empty streets of his imagination. 'Death for the sake of such happiness – for the sake of my body's bliss – well that would be a mere ... but my lands would be forfeit, lady,' he ended and cried by way of a plea, 'In perpetuity, madam!' for he was thinking of another perpetuity altogether, spent in the company of this devil's woman.

She took the sword out of his hand again and caressed his cheek as though he were a hysterical child in need of consolation.

'Barnard's a-hunting,' she whispered, 'and I hope he meets his death in the forest and never comes back to me. You have nothing to fear from him. Or his lady, either.' Her mouth came nearer, nearer still. He could smell the sweetness of cinnamon on her breath. She had been expecting all morning to kiss ...

Outside, a subhuman shriek was compounded with a wild, feathery ruffling – like the departure of the Christmas angels – Joan tumbled into the lobby and slammed the door behind her. Her back turned at first to the great hall, she was unaware of Musgrave and Elinor and shouted through the doorway, 'Truth's truth! Can't make it no other,' to which a pair of fists beat a reply on the door panel.

When she saw the two, standing staring at her from the centre of the room, she was still too outraged to be cautious:

'Yon bastard threw a duck at me,' she cried. 'H'm picked up a big fat duck an' heaved'm at me. Bastard. 'Fore God he's a bastard that one.' The door struck her as Geoffrey burst into the lobby.

'You dirty old liar, you're not worth trampling ... '

The four stood looking at each other – man and woman, woman and man, until Musgrave saw his opportunity and broke for the door.

'Believe me, madam, I would if I dared,' he said in the voice of a tradesman who has at long last foreclosed on credit. 'But God knows me for a coward.' He strode over the duck which had paddled, dazed, into the hallway behind Geoffrey, and walked across the yard at a pace which now and then broke into a run.

9

JOAN UNDERSTOOD SO MUCH from seeing so little that she felt
herself a gipsy again, seeing down the long dark corridors of
other people's lives into the unseen places of their future. She
had never *passed herself off* as clairvoyant, for what she knew,
she knew – from a face, a phrase, a pallor. She knew not to
comment on what she saw in Elinor. She bent and picked up
the duck and put it out through the door while Geoffrey poured
out accusations and spleen.

'She made such slanders on you, lady. She's wickeder than
the woman of Endor. She's wickedness itself. Bid me stop her
mouth that she tell no more of her filthy lies. It does you no
honour, lady, truly, to have kept her alive. Let me put a whip
to her, *please, lady*.' He had not been supplicant to so reticent a
madonna since he had stayed on his knees in the monastery a
whole afternoon while his mother was dying. He plunged
on – shouting down the gipsy, although the gipsy never once
interrupted him. 'And she ate, mistress. She ate on purpose to
defy you. She ate an apple off a cart. She stuffed her face and
she laughed and shamed God with her filthy bawdy tongue...'

'Did you eat, Joan?' asked the mistress in a thin, unintonated
voice that made the peasant woman's face twitch.

'Not the first time an apple betrayed we ladies, madam,' and
her cheekbone gathered the folds of her jowls into a desolate
leer.

'Lady? But you're not a lady, Joan,' said Elinor, in the same suppressed monotone. 'You're just a gipsy, isn't that right? Well? Isn't it?'

'I's your ladyship's good servant ma'am an' I delivered the message best I could and I didn't eat no food till your bidding was done.'

'You hadn't brought me word, Joan. You failed to bring me word. You broke our bargain.'

'She did,' said Geoffrey, punching the woman in the back so that she reeled. 'And now she'll give you over to the bailiff, witch.'

'And now I must give you up to the bailiff, as Geoffrey says. Yes. Yes.' She was thoughtful, partly aware, through her need for vengeance, of another need for Joan to be put out of the world's hearing.

'To be hung up high as high,' Geoffrey shrieked, seeing only that the dissolution of Joan would dissolve everything she had ever said.

'To be hanged, yes. I fear so,' said Elinor.

Joan looked from one to the other. They were like children tormenting a cat; the one, hysterical and shrill, might have let the creature escape as he hooted and danced about; the other was hysterical, but not in such a way that she would let go her grip on the poor cat's hide.

'Fetch the bailiff, Geoffrey.'

Joan sank down involuntarily on to her knees. It was as if her legs had followed Geoffrey as he ran off across the yard. A bright gleam touched her paralysed brain and stirred it towards survival. 'Bailiff's gone a-hunting, lady. Will come back with the master at his shoulder.'

'Geoffrey will find someone else,' Elinor replied. 'Tell me,

51

what message *did* you give Master Musgrave?'

'Clear as I could make it, lady. And didn't he come like an arrow from the bow? He burned for you, lady. I know no different and I know what I know. He burned like a torch at the name of you. Bless you, madam, didn't I say there was queer things said of Musgrave? He's maybe a man incapable; he's maybe of a different breed.'

Elinor was near to tears. If she gave way, there would be no one but Joan, faithful old Joan, to supply comfort. The gipsy began to get to her feet. 'There's plenty to love you deeper and better than little Robin Musgrave.'

The tears were swallowed up as if her lids were salt, and she caught Joan off balance as she rose, pushed her sprawling and stood over her with the longsword she still had in her hand. The double sheath she threw over the chest and it fell down between press and wall with a single slap of leather.

Geoffrey reached the bailiff's house without a thought passing through his head. No one answered his knocking except the chickens in the yard. Beside the lock-up he found the bailiff's son — a boy of twelve — playing with a puppy.

"Where's your father?'

'Gone to the hunt, master,' said the boy, chasing the puppy round the circular wall of the lock-up as it took fright of Geoffrey. 'What's the matter?'

'Gipsy trouble at the castle,' he panted, leaning his hands on his knees to catch his breath.

'What's that? Gipsies?' A grizzled old head appeared at the slit in the lock-up wall. 'Don't lock no gipsies up in here or we'll flay their hides off'm. We're both King's soldiers. Gipsies is it? Gipsies isn't fit to breathe the same air as a King's soldier.'

Another of the King's troop pushed his comrade out of sight and peered out at Geoffrey. He must have been twenty years out of active service. 'Need a helping hand, boy? Scourge of the land, gipsies. Thieving and murdering. Brought the evil eye to a barracks of mine once. Ten men dead before...'

'What are you in for?' Geoffrey panted.

'What? Buggered if I can remember, boy.'

His comrade called from somewhere beneath the slit, 'Drank so much last night it could have been anything.'

Geoffrey slid the bolts on the door and urged them out. They tottered into the street blinking in the daylight. One had lost an arm in France. The other was covered in traces of his drinking. They left a trail of straw behind them as they followed Geoffrey back towards the manorhouse.

On the way they gained the blacksmith, who brought a length of chain – as a weapon or restraint, who knew? – and a crowd of women whose jabbering gradually faded and left only the massed sweeping of their skirts along the ground.

At the head of this determined train Geoffrey skittered along, leaning forwards in his shoes, his shoulders hunched behind his purposeful head and his fists clenched. 'The Lady Barnard wishes it put a finish to instantly,' he exhorted them, though there began to be other, private thoughts in his head. If it were only possible to tell Elinor the precise slur Joan had cast on her honour there might be a reward of thanks better than gold. He had fought, as the old chivalric heroes had fought, to champion her good name, to defend her against infamy in the mouths of the ungodly. The duck he had thrown was, in certain respects, like a gauntlet thrown in the teeth of the infidel. In certain respects.

The swish, swish of the women's dresses and the last links

of the blacksmith's chain chinking along the ground began to impinge on Geoffrey's high romance. He was having to insert a skip at every fourth pace to keep ahead of the one-armed veteran. The loud thump of his own feet on the wooden drawbridge startled him to a standstill, but the crowd behind pressed past.

'It's only old Joan,' he murmured as the women clustered by the doorposts and the King's troopers and the blacksmith strode unhesitatingly in on their liege's lady and the Scourge of the Land.

Joan came out backwards, being drawn by her grey hair by the one-armed soldier. Most of the women spat on her in unison; some would not look at her closely enough to take aim, for fear of the evil eye.

Geoffrey was fascinated by the long rope of grey hair. There was something very private about an old woman's hair, always under its headcloths, always out of sight. But Joan was not old. Why should her hair be so grey? She caught hold of a woman's sleeve as she was handed through the crowd: 'M-y boy, my Jacky's sick with the croup, neighbour. See to him for sweet Jesu's sake.'

'Blasphemer! Egyptian!' the King's man shouted into her ear.

'It's 'is chest, neighbour,' she called as she was swept out of reach of the woman who, in the growing hysteria, pulled off her own, sullied, separate sleeve and threw it into the moat, spitting after it.

The prisoner began to protest her Christianity, but it was as though the community had found paganism, like a plague bubo, in their own armpit, and nothing could save them now but to shut themselves up with God, and lime a cross on the door.

'Baptise her!' someone shouted. 'Baptise'r bastard boy!'

'You know me for a Christian, masters!' she cried as she reached their shoulders. 'The People are Christians all!' she cried as she reached the length of their upright arms, like a bird caught in the uppermost forks of the lime trees. She made an angular V in the air as she hurtled into the water of the moat. Her reflection came up to meet her like the open jaws of some monstrous fish that gaped and swallowed and withdrew into the depths. Only after the space of two or three breaths did the water regurgitate her, head distorted to an unnatural length as she dropped her jaw for breath and the grey hair plastered her temples and cheekbones and congealed her head to her body. Feeling for a footing, she felt the silt swill in the hems of her dress and around her ankles, but there was no bottom to it and her clothes were filling with water. Lunging for a chain that hung down, fortuitous, under the bridge within reach, she clutched it in hands slippery with weed, and looked up into the face of the blacksmith, and felt his rage through all the length of his chain.

He pulled her up hand over hand, as though she weighed as little as a bucket, and set her down for her neighbours to refresh their fear. Their common voice was building higher and higher as they shouted down any misgivings. The woman, whose sleeve lay floating now in the water, had broken away from the main group and, surrounded by neighbours and conscripts, was striding purposefully away. Her place had been taken by others – men and girls in from the squat, short fields that fanned so meanly out from the village as to be never out of earshot. An incident, any incident, was so welcome in the interminable sameness of their long preordained, mudrooted lives – a cock-fight, a fair, a mumming, a hanging. They were spectators to a man. It took the King's men, three arms between them, and the blacksmith and the fuller and the idiot son of the priest to fetch Joan down to the churchyard and bundle her up into the tower's loft.

The hatch to the roof had grassed up and would not open except to the blacksmith. As Joan was pushed up, like some battle projectile, and her head burst into open air, she surfaced again as she had from the moat, this time out of the clammy cold of the brick loft into a blue patch of sky between clouds – a tessellated square of sky held in by the tower's four walls. Below in the churchyard a crop of round, brown faces ripened on stalky, foreshortened bodies. Geoffrey stood separate, beyond the yard wall.

'Geoffrey!' Joan called, because, of all the faces, it was the only one that had not habitually shunned her in her time at the manorhouse. The pink dish of his face shallowed until all she could see was the W of his receding hairline. 'Geoffrey!'

A pale pastel shape with sharp hands was cutting its way through the knots of gawping villagers. A thin, imploring voice reached as high as the tower roof. The oldest Fettimore girl was exhorting the rabble shrilly, insistently, that good Christians would never consider such a sin.

The priest arrived and there was a momentous pause as he pushed through the crowd and then as they listened to his feet scratching on the runged ladder of the tower.

'She's a gipsy, Father!' they called up from among the graves, like a matful of children.

Elizabeth Fettimore had faith in the priest. 'Father! Have them set that poor woman free,' she called. 'She's been in the service of Lady Barnard this long year past, and we all well know it!'

They rounded on her, incited by bloodlust. 'The lady herself delivered up the witch!'

'Then let me take her under my protection, Father! Under my family's protection!' Her voice broke; she was not accustomed to raising it above a demure whisper. She had to repeat herself, and could see the priest's face peering down, bewildered, hesitating. Why were all the men of authority away at the hunt, it seemed to say.

Joan, a creature of the People, had no reverent confidence in the clergy, or in Elizabeth. She suddenly conceived the notion of belittling her crime beside a much bigger and better sin.

''Tis only the Lady Elinor's lust for Little Musgrave that's brought me to this!' she bellowed over the low, castellated wall. 'And his for her! ... Tell'm Geoffrey! Tell'm how it is, for you surely know it for the truth.'

Geoffrey had gone. The eyes that swept about for him could not see him where he had crept to hide. Only Joan could see him, crouched between the buttress and the wall.

The priest knew then where his duty lay. He nodded his head sharply towards the pool of moat water at the gipsy's feet.

The idiot boy, having both his church's and his natural father's dispensation, bent and grasped Joan's calves in the circle of his arm and body, and launched her out over and away from the wall. The trajectory was so sharp that the crowd below her was forced to scatter where she landed.

10

LIKE A COMET, MUSGRAVE plunged from the bright heat of the manorhouse on to the heath in a wide, elliptical course which took him as far away as strength would carry him, then brought him irresistibly back.

Indifferent at first to what impact he had made on Elinor, he was gradually drawn into an urgent longing to know. Finally turning back off the heath towards his own house, he found his stride lengthening, his pace quickening, but in the direction of the manorhouse. He was like a thing thrown up into the air, falling back out of its zenith.

It seemed that if only he knew what reactions he had left behind him, a course of action would chart itself. He must know whether he had inflicted pain on Elinor. Of course, he told himself, such a lust as hers was so indiscriminate, so open-mouthed to swallow any and every man, that she was beyond injury. Superficial blemishes on her pride she could salve through some act of spite, some petty revenge worked on him through her husband. Musgrave would welcome it. But no deep hurt could penetrate to the small corrupt thing she wore in place of a heart. Surely.

Unable to satisfy himself fully with the argument, he was drawn back towards the house, thinking to clarify the situation with Joan, to discover how such a misunderstanding had come about, to interrogate his own soul for a trace of guilt. The reasons he found for the centripetal pull on his spirit were more than he could find words for, and none of them were true. He retraced his steps, searching the gravel for a reason as though it were a button or a dropped coin. But in fact he was searching for the scales which had dropped from his eyes.

Insight was an agony shifting inside him. In his inner emptiness, it crashed against his heart and rolled away again, and again crashed down on it. Insight had poured in at his eyes like molten lead, and, if he could have found the scales of ignorance there in the grass or the gravel, he would have clapped them over his eyes and recaptured his blind illusions about Elinor. He longed to be in love again.

On the heels of regret came temptation. What had she offered him that he had turned down with the disgust of an angel disparaging earthly food? What would he have seen had he dared to look, as Lot's wife dared, at the soul-stealing sights of Gomorrah?

With these thoughts on him, Musgrave collided with a little boy in shift and bare feet, running away from a crowd of women. His face, as he looked up at Musgrave, was unnaturally flushed.

For once, the women seemed too preoccupied with catching the child to treat Robin to their usual lecherous flattery. He held the thin shoulders until they took the boy from him, thanked him as if he had stopped some chicken for the cleaver, and dragged the child away in the direction of the manor.

Thieving? In his nightshirt? The child began to cough and wheeze with a rattle in his chest that Musgrave felt in his own. But it was not his concern, and he followed only because they were all moving towards the house, towards the magnetic north that drew his face always round towards it.

The glances cast back at Musgrave by the women were so covert that he began to be interested: patently, his presence embarrassed them. Why were they taking the boy to Elinor, crossing on to the drawbridge with him as if they would march directly inside? Instead of doing so, they threw the child round from grip to grasp until one woman's frenzy was sufficient to lift him and throw him, screaming, into the moat.

A wash of darkness lapped up round the base of Musgrave's brain. As the little white figure surfaced, its white rag of clothing transparent and a little bony hand clawing at the sky, the walls of Musgrave's lungs began to adhere to his backbone. He was running before he knew it and shouting, though he could not take his eyes off the boy to fix on the women. 'For Christ's sake. For Jesu Christ!' Then his lungs were empty and would not refill.

One of the women had got hold of a shepherd's crook and seemed to be going to extend it to the boy. But as its ramshorn came to rest on his shoulder she pushed him under and the green water swirled over his open mouth.

'In nominay parti!' she bawled.

'Ought you say that, Maggie?' said another, but Maggie shrugged her off and looked for the child whom she had forgotten to let up in struggling after her Latin. 'In nominay filly!' He went under again, his hands still gripping the crook above the water but the horn's U resting across his throat.

Musgrave tore the crook out of the woman's hands and threw it over the other side of the bridge. She looked at him aggrieved, irritated, and her mouth struggled on through, 'In nominay spirito sanctuary ...' He planted a hand on her forehead and pushed her backwards.

'Get him out!'

'He's a gipsy's pagan boy,' they chimed in unison.

'Get him out!'

'We're baptising him, master.'

'Get him out!'

The veins in his neck and temples were visibly marking his heartbeat: they watched it with vacant, unrepentant eyes, blinking in time with his snatched, ineffectual breaths. His windpipe was as flat as a reed.

'Get him out now!'

'How's it to be done, master?'

Musgrave looked down at the water which licked the house wall lasciviously, lapping towards him, gaping to swallow him. And the boy stretched both hands in the air and sank like a white wafer sliding down a gullet.

The women had not thought beyond swamping the boy in his redemption. The moat was six feet below the bridge and they in their wool dresses and pendulous headcloths. Men did not fear water. Men did not lose their breath irrevocably on the brim of a domestic moat. Already their eyes had burdened him with the responsibility of getting Joan's boy out.

'He's drowning, master,' they pointed out, with due respect for his rank. He bent down and they hurried to help him off with his boots, then the leather waistcoat. Women, whose sole ambition had been to finger his hair and brush against his skin, were loath to touch him now, the spittle white on his beard and his throat gouged out by some subcutaneous devil. He was drowning on behalf of the boy.

Stepping off the lift bridge, he saw his face reflected in a pitted wave, deformed and white-eyed – the face of his father that day they fetched him out of the well feet-first,

He plummeted into animate cold that clasped his chest, roared in at his ears, flooded in at his nose and mouth until he was water inside, water outside and his skin as open as a fishing net. Fish swam through him, the red bloodworms in the silt would colonise his eyes. But his hands had hold of the boy, and the child was buoyant.

No panicking desire to breathe made him clutch at the surface, for he knew that he could no more breathe in air than in water. He was a pipeless amphibean floundering towards the end of one sealed lungful of breath. His feet touched the splaying buttress at the foot of the house wall, and he thrust the child up through the mirrory surface.

The women on the bridge gave a sort of weak cheer, then Elinor appeared on the plank bridge, floating against Musgrave's sky like a water lily.

'What's happening here? Who's in the water? Why don't you move?' His cheek pressed to the wall, Musgrave watched her lively dumbshow, his ears deafened with water. 'Something wooden! A pole! A ladder!' She spread one hand at Musgrave and the child as if to beg their patience, and ran inside, dragging women after her by the hand, by pieces of their garments.

The child began to struggle in Musgrave's arms who felt his feet slither off the buttress and the pointing crumble at his fingertips. The boy beat him about the head and he returned its staring hatred dumbly, feeling like old St Christopher beaten down by the great weight of his child God.

He tried to remember the rudiments of swimming from a childhood spent far back from banks, and as the wall slithered treacherously out of his grasp, he keeled towards the bridge, curving one arm unconvincingly into a stroke.

'Robin, take hold!' Elinor's voice called through the water, and a massive wooden bench crashed down like a felled tree beside his head. It plunged down and perhaps sank itself in the black silt but did not resurface. It was followed by a chair, an ornate painted chair which caught him a blow on the shoulder and, when the child's hands reached for it, sank deep under him. Another bench and a table from the lobby were heaved off the bridge in a bombardment which Musgrave experienced surreally from under the water, his ears deafened by the blood ringing in them, his face seemingly pushed concave by the water rushing from under the plunging furniture.

'You can't swim, master,' said the boy, floating away from Musgrave on the chairback, watching him with recriminating, bloodshot eyes. Robin clung to a bench, rolled under it as it rolled in the water, straddled it with his legs and arms and rolled again, against the mud bank of the moat. The table, with its lion feet in the air, laid its back on the bank for a ladder. The muddy water escaped through his hose. A woman said, 'Lord, what a body he has on him,' and her friends giggled nervously. They pulled him out by the hands and laid him alongside Joan's little boy.

The child began to cough and continued without pause to cough while, for Musgrave, the line would not be drawn between the child's wind and his own. He listened for the coughing to ease and a breath to slip by into his own vacuum-empty chest.

'Is he drowned?' said a woman.

'So quick?' said another.

'Nay,' said another, 'It's his way to fall down in a fit like he was a drowned man. His spirit's with his father.'

'He's wrestling with the Dead.'

Their words fell like stones on Musgrave as he wrestled on

his back for breath, his feet braced against the ground and his hips arched up. And his head driving into Elinor Barnard's stomach.

'Carry the child in and set him to bed beside the fire,' she said to a peasant woman, '— tell one of the servants to bank it up. Go and fetch his mother to him — you'll maybe find her in the lock-up.' One turned to go. 'Oh, and if she says she won't come, tell her she's not to be afraid of me. Tell her why she's to come.'

No one in the crowd knew to disabuse her, but having delivered the child into the great hall they returned and stood about at a distance, to see if Musgrave's spirit would wrest itself free of his father's.

His hips had relaxed on to the grass and the arch of his knees had fallen apart so that one leg lay at an angle along the ground. It was beginning to rain, but his head was turned sideways in Elinor's lap and he was breathing hard but slowly through a thick blanket of sleep. His pale lids with their blue veining looked as if they were transparent and let through the colour of his eyes. When religion spoke of the scales falling from a man's eyes, they were surely scales such as these.

11

In the churchyard nobody moved.

They all had their separate memories of spitting on Joan in the street or turning her boy off their gardens; of selling her a chicken or buying a pitcher of manorhouse wine, unofficial like, from the kitchen door; or making a late-night call at the filthy little house for a little piece of People's advice. Some of the older men could remember other visits, other reasons. A gipsy was gone from the community like a cock's incessant crowing when suddenly one morning its head is off and there's nothing to disrupt sleep. Nothing to disrupt sleep. Nothing, to disrupt sleep.

Elizabeth Fettimore grasped the monk by his surplice as he swept out of the tower door. 'I shall tell my uncle of this,' she said. 'And Lord Barnard will know of it.' The priest pulled away from her and hurried through the crowd in the direction of the monastery refectory and anonymity. He did not pause to make the sign of the cross over Joan and without it no one would touch her. She remained in the churchyard, laid out like discarded peel.

'Peel with your right hand and throw it over your right shoulder,' she had said to Geoffrey when he asked whom he would marry. But he had gone to look at the peel on the floor and deciphered no letter – nothing as legible as the first letter of a Christian or surname, and he had ground the peel underfoot, then thrown it into the pig run. Joan lay here distinctly legible, bent round into the P of her gipsy Peder's name, and Geoffrey could not put the incident of the apple peel out of mind as he stood and looked down at her.

'You boy. You work at the manorhouse, don't you?'

He looked up at Elizabeth Fettimore but could recall neither her name nor the context of her face.

'Is Robin Musgrave up there now? Don't just gawp at me, boy. Is he? Is he there?'

'No mistress. It wasn't true.' He struggled back towards comprehension. 'She lied. There was no truth in it. There's no love between my lady and the Little Musgrave. Nor worse.'

Elizabeth was repelled by his small stony eyes and the liquid bulging of his body through his clothes. As he wept, his cheeks shook like meat in aspic. 'Nor worse!' he shouted at her and with one last look at Joan spelling out her disastrous fortune on the ground, he sagged away from her, falling heavily on each fat haunch in turn.

Rain broke off the wooded hills and trailed wraithlike towards the village. As its first drops swelled to a hissing, it confused and melded together the whispered voices that surrounded Elizabeth.

'Musgrave's about his business again...'

'... away at the hunting...'

'... comes of a lonely young wife...'

'... ought to be cut off at's roots...'

'... going to tell his lordship?'

'... believe no ill of her. Nobody'll...'

'... best be gone by cock crow!' Even a loud guffaw of male laughter was smudged into the hiss of closing rain. Elizabeth shook violently with an inner cold; she was nauseous with the

66

growing taint of Musgrave's name as it was passed from one reeking mouth to the next.

'Robin,' she said, to see if it tasted as sweet as ever in her own mouth. 'Oh, Robin, it isn't true. God forbid it to be true, my own love.'

'... sweet enough cause to die...' hissed the rain and the voices '... but he won't be towsling no angels in the next world...' She drew her skirts close round her legs. '... only lady devils...' and ran towards Robin's stone house on the corner of the village. If he were there she would fall down at his feet and beg forgiveness for this corrupt village, writhing with tongues like a body in its corruption, writhing with maggots.

But she would beg him to arm himself with an alibi and witnesses: the words of a pagan gipsy woman that should have washed away in the rain might just stick like tar to his good name now that the gipsy was dead.

Elinor sat on the window seat holding his two boots clutched to her breast and rocking forward and back. Her eyes were turned on the view over the valley, but clearly she was unaware even of the torrential rain.

Musgrave watched her through his lashes, pretending still to be asleep where they had laid him on her bed. Her dress stood on the floor, slumped but upright within the muddy circle of its hem; she still had on her green velvet sleeves over the white shift. Strands of wet hair were sticking to the back of her neck and the braided plaits were dishevelled, uncoiling.

Presently she got up and crossed to the bed. He shut his lids and watched her instead through the million staring pores of his skin as she unlaced his doublet gingerly – in the hope of not waking him. She loosened his belt and he heard her shush

67

under her breath as the buckle clanked on to the cover. Drops of moisture fell on him but, without opening his eyes, he could not judge whether they were off her hair.

'Oh Robin,' she whispered, expressing the weariest disappointment and depression. 'Oh *Robin*.' He had heard the tone in mothers' voices when children too young to be held responsible had wrought some irremediable damage.

She peeled the revers of his shirt back off his chest: Musgrave could judge how chilled his body was by the warmth of her touch, though he thought, in all, that he had never been so comfortable in his whole life. Her hand was on his thigh: he could feel that she was faced with a dilemma. He opened his eyes, but she did not notice, chewing her lip, her hand involuntarily tightening on his leg.

'What? Have you never unfastened a cod-piece before, lady?'

She jumped so violently that he sat up and caught hold of her by the arms — apologising without being apologetic. The trembling incited him; her confusion fascinated him. She turned her head entirely away from him.

'How old are you?' he asked and she replied 'Eighteen,' twice, since her voice deserted her the first time.

'And what did you want of me?'

'Nothing.'

'This morning?'

'Oh, this morning,' Eventually she turned her face so that he moved into the rim of her vision, and said, 'You're famous, Robin Musgrave.'

'You're wrong, Elinor Barnard. The women hereabouts make much of little.'

She pulled out of his grip. 'Is love such a little matter, then?'

'You mistake me, madam. There's a deal of lust and a deal of covetousness in this town, but love? I couldn't say. It's a thing people keep to themselves. I've received none that I know of.'

'Dirty Mary loves you – and Belper's old wife – and Liza Fettimore...'

'Liza? Surely not.'

'... and Anne and Grisel and Martha. Dirty Mary says you're like Cain and Abel both together.'

'Love's not kept in a cod-piece, lady. And if it were...' He was vexed; there were names there to which he could not even put a face. Strangers, total strangers had staked claims on his body, leaving him in ignorance. Even Samson, waking shorn, had known the woman responsible!

'Joan calls you an un-natural man.'

A sudden memory jarred on Musgrave. 'Why was her child thrown in the moat?'

'What?'

'Why was Joan's boy thrown into the moat?'

'He fell in. Surely. Nobody would throw a child into a moat. He has a weak chest. I fear for him. I wish his mother would come to him.'

'So do I,' he replied. 'She's a good soul. A heathen and a whore, I suppose, but a good soul. Truly, I welcome Joan's opinion of me for an un-natural man – more than any compliment Dirty Mary pays me.'

'Oh, Dirty Mary only said...'

'I know full well what she said: she's recounted nights to me that I know for a Christian I spent in my own bed, in my own company.' He interrupted himself with his own thoughts. 'You've no knowledge of unfastening a cod-piece!' he exclaimed, taking hold of her shoulders again so tightly she squealed with fright. 'Your head's as full of sins as the confessional: you've

69

everyone's sins but your own in there!'

She turned her head down and away from him, like a little vetch flower too heavy for its stem. 'But I'm not un-natural, though, really I'm not. I want things like other women.'

Musgrave was possessed by the thought of the alabaster angels, in the church, basted with the sins of Dirty Mary and Belper's old wife; and while dispensing clemency and absolution, learning all the dirty words and conceiving a gradual, nagging envy.

Poor, stupid angels. Better keep to their cold, draughty niches and let the words trickle like guano over the outside only of their heads.

'Poor lonely angels,' said Musgrave, taking her head between his hands.

This is how the devil, he thought — this is how the devil draws sinners off the brink of the world. Not with gaffs and grapples or with claws that rend them limb from limb, but with his fingers in their hair and the heels of his hands feeling a little pulse of fright in their throat and, with a gentle downward embrace, shutting out their light as he draws their face down to his loins.

12

Hurrying to get out of the rain, Geoffrey was almost across the lift bridge before he saw the furniture floating in the moat. Already upset, it only unsettled him more to see the bulky feet of a bench hail him from the water and the long trestle from the lobby taking root in the silty bank. A chair had been pulled out: it stood braving the rain on the grass. He picked it up and was carrying it inside when a voice called and a woman hurried up the path signalling to him. She wanted access to the Lady Barnard and showed signs of distress.

'What do you want with the mistress?'

'She sent me to fetch the gipsy to her boy – who's in the castle. But she's dead. Madam said she'd be in the lock-up but she's dead in the churchyard and no one paying her any heed.'

'The lady had no idea ...' said Geoffrey, concealing the question in his words.

'You knew?'

'I was in the area.'

'But what's to be said to the boy? Who's to have him? He's inside on the settle.'

'Arrangements will be made,' said Geoffrey, edging himself and the bulky chair through the door but firmly excluding her.

The boy looked up at him from the settle by the fire with dull, indifferent eyes and coughed wetly. Geoffrey took a mental note of furniture missing from the lobby and the great hall and

71

wondered if it was an indication of some struggle Joan had put up *before* the lynch mob arrived. The whole subject was untenable, so he put it out of mind with one more manful effort and passed through to the service end of the house.

Joan's trug, full of rosemary and wild garlic, was hanging from a hook under the ladder. The thoughts boorishly filed into his mind and stood demanding attention.

Just how much damage had Joan done with her lying against his mistress? He would be glad if Robin Musgrave became somehow sullied with Joan's fall from the tower and was put out of the way; Geoffrey had no time for these pretty, fleshless men with their pretentious, chimneyed houses. Sheets: he probably had sheets. There was room for only one chimneyed roof, one pair of sheets in a feudal society. Sheets bred lasciviousness in the lower orders.

Another sequence of thoughts was put out of his mind. Geoffrey sat down on his mattress, hugging his knees. He got up and eased his lady's shift out from under the palliasse and, putting it around his shoulders so not a grain should drop, set the mill of his imagination grinding.

Suppose Elinor had needed Musgrave's help or advice on a matter of great delicacy. Suppose that, unknown to Geoffrey with his modest lack of ambition, Elinor had formed a passion so violent for him, for Geoffrey, that she had conceived a desperate notion to free herself of the Lord Barnard. After all, she had given him signs and signals beckoning him and, like a fool, he had not acted on these. Besides, he didn't so much as own a sword, so that a man of experience would be essential to the overall plot. Suppose, then, that Joan had been sent to summon Musgrave – a potential assassin, no more – to a woman deranged with immoderate desire for someone else entirely. All in all Geoffrey, as the object of her passion, felt unable to judge Elinor harshly for such outlandishness.

Fortunately, the Little Musgrave had refused her, hadn't he? He had said, 'I would if I dared, madam, but God knows me for a coward,' and run out of the house. (He was in possession of too dangerous a knowledge: he would have to be disposed of.) Poor Joan, for misreading the situation so completely and being caught between archer and butt. It all came down to whether Geoffrey dared or did not dare to murder the Lord Barnard himself.

Elizabeth Fettimore was standing at the foot of the ladder, calling up softly.

'What do you want?' he said from his hands and knees, frowning down through the hatch.

'I want Robin Musgrave,' she said, emphasizing each quiet word. 'He's not at his house.'

'Well, he's not here. I told you already.'

'I think he is, young man. His jacket's wet beside the fire.'

'He was out with a hawk early on. On the heath,' Geoffrey insisted.

'And the little boy says Robin was fetched in from the moat along with him and is in the Lady Elinor's room. If you aren't afraid for Musgrave, you might fret for your mistress. There have been words said that can't be unsaid.'

'You evil-minded woman,' he snapped through the hatch like a dog barking. She lifted an arm and slapped him sharply across the nose.

'Those over you will crush you underfoot for the slug you surely are,' she said in her quick, sedate whisper. 'It matters not what *is*, but only what *seems*. There must be no bad meat on the Lord Barnard's plate when he gets back from the hunting.

And there are those in the village would put it there just to see what happens.'

'You love the Little Muckrake, don't you,' he sneered, but was too slow to avoid another blow on the nose. 'Go and look for yourself! Go on! Knock at her door – you'll find it out soon enough. Musgrave's not here!'

Below him, her face flushed a vivid red. 'I would do, boy.'

'Well? But?'

She pursed her lips and breathed in deeply, clenching her skirts in her fists. 'But I fear what I'd find, you stupid, arrogant little speck. And I won't shame the Little Musgrave with my person.'

She turned and went back into the great hall where he could hear her talking to the gipsy boy, urging him into his clothes, taking responsibility for him with efficiency until she had time and heart to do so with tenderness.

When she had gone, Geoffrey went and lay face down on his bed with the shift under him and he was still in this position when Elinor's voice called him from the far end of the upper floor.

'Geoffrey,' she said, meeting him outside the chamber door in only the green sleeves of her dress over her smock. Her face was sunrise bright. She put the fingertips of her right hand on his chest as she spoke and looked him intently in the eye so that his bowels melted with lust. All his imaginings were incontrovertibly true. 'Geoffrey, I have a most especial duty for you to perform,' she said. Involuntarily he put his hand to his crotch, afflicted by rapture. 'Listen,' she confided. 'I wish you to keep watch at the gallery window. All night. And to call me at once if my lord's hunting party should come in sight. At once.

Do you understand? I want to be sure to welcome him fittingly. Anyone. Announce anyone that comes.'

He swallowed. 'I understand. I think I do. I understand. Within hearing of you calling me.'

'Well . . .' she said doubtfully.

'And I'm to "cut off" his lordship.'

Her smile was incendiary. 'You're wiser than I took you for, my darling Geoffrey. You understand exactly,' and, touching his cheek, she withdrew into her chamber, opening the door so narrowly that she seemed to slip through like spilled candlelight.

It was dark on the landing after that. The sky was a bubonic green with rain and imminent nightfall.

Geoffrey hung strappadoed between reality and fantasy, swinging to face the torrential valley and then the chamber door and then the valley again. All the while his ears let by the murmur of two soft voices, he imagined himself lying in wait for his liege lord, striking him dead in his saddle and setting the horse loose, to lose its burden on the heath while he, Geoffrey, crept into Elinor's sheeted bed and into his Elinor's urgent embrace.

It was the sound of his prayers, that was all.

Geoffrey de Stoke d'Abernon he would be, and be done with inferior Saxony which bred nothing but his blond hair. Musgrave had contemptible Saxonish hair. Geoffrey de Stoke d'Abernon and be done with centuries of serfdom.

Just one look as his lover put off her sleeves, gathered up her smock and climbed into his future bed, and he would lay to rest that one nagging doubt that kept dragging his star out of the ascendant. One look at what was promised him and the spectre of George Barnard might fatten up in his imagination into a killable beast. He sagged down on his knees beside the big iron keyhole and the draught through it jabbed him sharply in the eye.

He watched from beginning to end, Creation to Chaos. He watched the sibilant serpent raise its hooded head in Eden and Eve's mouth gorge on the fruit. He saw the treasures of Israel melt into a sweaty, heaving liquor of pale gold and raise up again hard into a loathsome beast on all fours with worship heaped on its ungodly, golden head. He saw how water flowed where Moses struck with his conjuror's rod. He saw Samson's rotting lion, its bowels oozing honey. He saw Sisera take revenge on Jael for the tent peg driven deep into his dreams; and Jezebel was hurled down out of the windows of his imagination and smooth-furred dogs strained over her with saliva loose in their mouths. He saw David dance lewd at the profaned holy altar and saw Absalom hanging by his long leafy hair while the arrows of Saul plunged into his vulnerable, jerking body. He heard the Song of Solomon like a man stone deaf. He saw the transformation of Nebuchadnezzar into a brute animal drenched in dew. He saw the Gadarene pigs tumble down on top of one another in ecstasies of madness at the bottom of the cliff.

Revealed through the dirty keyhole, the vile angel with his gilded measuring rod finally took full measure of the golden city, and all the gross apocalyptic beasts lay panting on their flanks. Then Geoffrey wept and no one wiped away the tears: he wept all the saltwater of the combined oceans, until there was finally no more sea.

So he crawled to the stairhead on his hands and knees and sat on the top step governing his breath. Behind the lobby door he paused to choose the finest and heaviest of Barnard's cloaks; only when he pulled it round him did he realise that he was still

76

draped in the stolen shift and tear it off with clammy, scrabbling fingers and throw it into the fireplace.

The strappado on which he had hung between imagination and the truth broke loudly somewhere behind his head and he plunged into a dark, envious quagmire of mud and illusionless, filthy night.

13

His hopes of finding the Lord Barnard's hunting party at night in the primordial forest would have seemed futile if he had stopped to consider them. Strange, because hysteria made him realistic in other respects. How could he, a stupid, obese, slow-moving peasant keep his hand from shaking for long enough to kill Musgrave and Elinor where they lay? Why should he risk the gibbet, in any case, for the sake of a pair of coupling beetles? Barnard's revenge would encompass his and be above the law: it would be certain and bloody, untempered by wistful, ridiculous, adolescent dreams of ... His thoughts turned back and went another way. He was like a fly beating against a glass window with the sky beyond it.

The need for a horse impinged on him when, for the third time, he fell over on the track between the manorhouse and the village. He was scarcely beyond the midden for he could hear the click and whirr of its chrysalid and pupating life through the darkness. He looked to turn back to the stables, but they were almost within scope of the jaundiced candlelight from the upstairs room – and besides, all the horses would have gone to the hunting.

Musgrave's stables had horses in them. But the lights of his house were out and standing where it did, sunk in a hollow, with its roof below the skyline, nothing showed of its slate roof with its peculiar extrusion of a chimney. To find it, he would have to go down to the village and out again.

His feet and legs began to tell him that it was preposterous for a man of his build to run at all, let alone attempt the distance he had covered today. His thighs were chafed, and his hose had bobbled with the friction so that at every pace the threads caught and snagged. He was becoming web-legged.

There was a fight in progress inside the lock-up, although the door stood open. It stopped as the sound of his running feet approached, and began again when he was past, with a dull, syncopated thump and grunt.

He went down again outside the Belpers' house – the first in the town. One of Belper's strumpet daughters was laughing in the upper room. His hands found the start of the kennel, so he was midway across the street. Lucky he had fallen where he did or he might have stepped in the gulley and broken an ankle as he ran. He crawled to the house wall opposite and felt his way as far as the cross-street that led past the Fettimore cottage to Musgrave's and Exton's houses. Only when the darkness washed up the street towards him from the unlit limits did he realise that tallow lights did illuminate the village's windows here and there and that outside it – between it and the even darker forest – lay cubic acres of solid dark.

The Fettimores had horses. Two were hobbled outside the garden; they champed and stamped and breathed through fleshy, rolled lips, and, because he could not see where they began or ended, they massively barred his way. A swishing tail touched him in the darkness like a whip, and he blurted out that it had hurt him.

Unpremeditatedly, he found himself at the rear door of the Fettimore house, rattling it. Mother Fettimore opened to him, crossed herself at the sight of him, and tried to close the door.

But he burst in on her and was asking for Elizabeth, capable of anything but removing the manic grin distorting his face.

'She's a-bed. She's not here,' the terrified mother insisted, but Geoffrey pushed past her and met with Elizabeth's bare feet half-way up the stepladder.

'Give me a horse,' he grinned, letting her down into the room.

'How dare you come here? What devil's in you? Have your wits left you?'

'No, no. You were right about Musgrave! Give me a horse. Now, this second!' He was strong. His grip on her forearms put Elizabeth in fear of her own and her mother's life. She could perhaps safeguard her mother.

'Go and saddle a horse, mama,' she said, trying to press her thoughts into her mother's head. 'This gentleman's a foot-page at the manorhouse.'

'Foot-page, yes. Foot-page. How far shall I get on foot? I must have a horse. I must find Barnard, do you see? They're up there now, swiving and sweating – larding each other with damnation. And I'll bring it on them both soon enough if I can find the lord and master.'

'Jesus forgive and protect them,' said Elizabeth, and her mother said 'Amen' and left the door ajar as she stumbled out under the weight of a saddle.

'You can't find anyone tonight, boy. Wait till morning light,' Elizabeth argued, thinking to blind and lame every horse in the village before dawn.

'Gorging and fornicating,' he grinned involuntarily, holding on to her wrists until her hands were throbbing with blood. 'You were absolutely right. I'm sorry not to have believed you, mistress. Holding her like this and pressing home over and over ...' Both his arms were round her and the mud on him squeezed through her shift and trickled down her abdomen. With all her strength she could not push him away.

'Do you wish him dead for the sin of loving? What good does it do Barnard to know?'

'Good? To cut 'em to pieces and feed the pigs with'm!'

'You can only pain him and then he'll make you suffer for it, too. Why do you want them to suffer? What have they done to you?' She bent so far over backwards that her shoulders were on the bedding on top of the brick stove: his saliva ran down her neck. She took hold of what strands of hair she could find in the nape of his neck and banged his head on the stove.

'Anything. You'd do anything to save Muckrake's poxy body, wouldn't you? Waiting in line, aren't you, for his poxy favours, aren't you? Think you can even pocket me up in your placket out of harm's way. Try it, lady. Try if you can't keep me entertained.'

'Let go! Leave me be! Do what you like. Take a horse. Tell Barnard. He'll make you rich for it. But leave go of me, I beg you.'

He focussed on her, eased his grip, and a look came into him that might have stood in Legion's eyes when he was dispossessed of his last possession – his agony of devils. Even they might have kept a man company who faced a journey through acres of darkness into loveless forest.

When he had gone, Elizabeth's mother re-appeared in the doorway. 'I saddled a horse for him, daughter, But I'm afraid of the consequences if he finds the Lord Barnard. I'm afraid for the boy if he doesn't and goes astray in the forest. He's mad as April. Alas for those poor young things up at the castle. Their lives are forfeit with or without him.'

81

'What a man doesn't know ...' said Elizabeth without conviction.

'I meant their *eternal* lives my love. When adulterers have each other they have no need of God and God has no need of them.'

'I'm going out, mama,' said Elizabeth, climbing the stepladder to fetch her dress. 'I'd better tell you now that I loved the Little Musgrave: my goodness is still in thrall to him.'

Had she been empowered still to think beyond the pictures Geoffrey had daubed in her mind, she might have wondered at her mother making no attempt to stop her.

Her mouth against his cheek kissed gently and thoughtlessly, like an anenome kissing at the water.

'And have you never felt the like of this for your husband?' Musgrave asked, feeling the night could not pass without him asking. 'It's no small source of amusement in the town to see how he dotes on you.'

She opened her eyes, digested his question slowly and turned onto her back. 'People laugh at him. Well, I laugh at him too. Ha, ha. He's old and he smells of horse.' She was silent for a long time and Musgrave felt his spirit shrinking away from her like the shell of a chestnut. But then she said, 'I was given him like a horse. My mother told me of it three weeks before the marriage. George had been to a horsefair in Esher and on his way back he met Father out hunting. They drank one bottle, then they drank another – and then he fetched George back to our house to view me. Father came scurrying into the house like a fieldmouse out from under the beaters, and he told me to put on my fine dress and unbraid my hair. Then I'd to walk up and down a lot, pouring drinks and fetching off milk bowls and

82

so on. Like a serving wench. And George was right pleasant and said brave things on the wine. And after he'd gone, my mother said it was all concluded, and the letters started coming from George. Pretty letters. I think he wrote so well he wrote himself into a passion.

'My father – not like George – he can't write a word. Oh, he's master of two thousand acres, truly, and born to them, but he can't write two words above his name. So when he wrote to George, a letter for my mother to carry with her when she brought me over for the wedding, he spoke it out for my mother to write down. And I heard this letter spoken out. Good letters to bad purposes, I thought.

'Mother had told him I was nervous and shy. So he told George to drink me drunk on my wedding day to put me at my ease, so to speak. You see, he'd seen it done to good effect when I had a tooth go bad in me and needed it pulled, and he was taken with it for an idea. Hearing this letter read out, I had it fixed in mind not to drink a drop for fear of losing the memory of the day. The girls in the village – we were always talking ... love and marriage and beds and such things. But poor, stupid George, he took it for a local custom from my part of the world. Besides which he must have held it for a good idea in the light of other virgins of his knowing. And I was made to toast this and drink to that – a glass for every member of my wretched family – till I was green and nearly insensible. And George drank too. Well, he could hardly do else than drink, when he was toasting my relatives. And he was washed away by it too, in the end.

'They shut us up in this big, cold chamber. A rat had got up on the top,' – and she lifted a hand and pointed up at the roof of the bed – 'and George had out his sword and was hacking

83

at it till it fell down behind the bedhead and ran off, and him still smacking his flat sword down on the roof ...

'Well, the wine drowned all the Christian in me and I was bitter cold. And I begged him to show me love for what it was. And he flew into the most terrible drinking rage and said that young women shouldn't marry old men and expect a miracle — and wept tears and fell asleep.' She raised herself on one elbow and looked Musgrave in the face. 'And I remembered, the next morning, and George didn't. I remembered that he was more afraid than me, and after that I knew well enough how to please him. I told him I had made a vow of abstinence to St Friedeswide in gratitude for our marriage. And I know how he likes to see other men want what they can't have, and I draw their eye: I do that much. Then I listened to my women and the women in the church and I heard what they said about you and Love, and I saw you for myself. And after that all I could see was George's big soft belly and his shrivelled-up skin. I was afraid this morning when you ran away. I thought it was George all over again. But it wasn't. It wasn't.' Then she sank back on the pillows, smiling.

Musgrave turned his head from side to side on the pillow and thought of Barnard deprived of this orchid maidenhead by one small surfeit of wine. He must lie here, where Musgrave was lying, like a swaddled baby or a corpse in its shroud, bound immobile in the luxury of his imported linen sheets. This ignorant girl had served up Barnard's bliss to a stranger and fed the good old man on a crust and a smile. (Old? He was not even old.) How many years more would she pleasure Barnard with relentless purity and by flirting with other men? Fewer years than months; fewer hours than minutes.

'Washed away all the Christian in you, you said,' he recollected, as if it was all he had taken in of her story.

'Oh, the wine? Yes.'

'And do you still hope for salvation?' he asked mockingly.

'It's here, Musgrave, isn't it? All of mine. No, of course I don't look for salvation. Adulterers go to hell.'

It was Musgrave's turn to rise up on one elbow and look her in the face. She had heard it in church: it had crept to her through the lattice of bawdry and gossip and half-truths and whole lies and, along with the rest, it was to her incontrovertibly true.

'Then you're as afraid as me!' he said.

'When I'm alone,' she agreed. 'But I'm not alone at present.' Then she put her hand round the nape of his neck. 'You mustn't be afraid, Robin, for I love you with all my heart and soul.'

14

THE WHITES OF THE HORSE'S EYES flared at Geoffrey through the darkness and it seemed to be searching out his foot with its hooves. He caught hold of a stirrup and felt his way in towards the flank, but the animal began to circle round and round him like Kraken circling a ship.

Horses had no part in his life: he could have gone forty years and not coveted a journey on horseback. Round and round he hopped on one foot-page's foot with the other foot-page's foot a yard short of the stirrup. A man came to fit what clothes he was given: his clothes and his habits hobbled him to his role in life and it was not Geoffrey's role to climb aboard vicious, obdurate horses inside the very tent of night. He reached one toe into the stirrup, the horse pulled away, his hose split, his hopping and the horse's hooves made sucking noises in the deepening mud.

His hatred overflowed. It enveloped the horse and the house and leeched on to Elizabeth Fettimore so that she became the chiefest ally of the filthy night, ranging herself between him and the successful destruction of Musgrave and the whore. She had only to accomplish the journey to the castle to warn them: he had to accomplish the impossible, with co-operation from nothing so much as a horse. He would have to prevent her: a woman's lust would drive her to preposterous lengths ...

Elizabeth, her cloak filling and rattling in the wind the moment she stepped out of the house, closed the door behind her. Following, Geoffrey let her get as far as the garden wall then grabbed hold by the hood and dragged her over backwards. She managed to break the cloak's fastening and ran back towards the door, clutching her throat. But he had hold of the wool of her skirt; she ran into its hems and went down like a rabbit in a gin.

'Jesu Hominum Salvator ...'

'Stop!' he hissed.

'... illuminatio mea ...'

'Quiet!' He picked up a chalk boulder that shone luminous near his hand and held it over her head as the weight of his body pinned her to the ground. 'Thought to warn them, did you? They're too busy to take heed of you, mistress. You come with me instead.'

'For Christ's sake, leave me be! Leave us all be!'

'I do my duty to the Lord Barnard and so must you, too. You come with me into the forest and you can help me find them out. He'll maybe make you rich for it,' he jeered into her ear as he lifted her – in a series of lifts as with a big, heavy chair – towards the snuffling horse.

Still brandishing the rock, he told her to get up on the horse which she led automatically to a mounting block against the side wall. Impelled by necessity, Geoffrey was on the block beside her in a second, and they climbed into the saddle together, she in front. Barnard's cloak was snarled up with the stirrup and saddle and legs, and wet horse struck up cold through the tear in his gusset. He was minded of the execution of witches, rolled downhill in a barrel full of nails, for he seemed to be astride just such a barrel as it rolled one way then another under his

87

inflexible, hair-pricked thighs, and Elizabeth's sobs came back to him on the wind.

There was only one likely place for Barnard's hunting party to have entered the forest; they had first to cross the river, and would do so at the most convenient, shallow place. By five in the morning, it would be getting light and if he were across the river by then it would leave only the shortest distance and the most difficult search to accomplish by early morning light. What a strategist he was becoming in this newly declared war of his against hell and its spawn! What unprecedented note Barnard would take of his obscure little foot-page!

A badger standing on its hind legs became suddenly visible, looking like a dwarfed Dominican pointing out the way. For a minute or more Geoffrey shook uncontrollably with terror while his self-disgust and hysterical fury swelled like a cyst and filled all the cavity of his imagination. In his inescapable role of a cowardly, un-noted foot-page, he leaned forward and eased his wrath by biting the Fettimore woman on the shoulder.

He was the antler and Elinor the fur upon it. He shed her painlessly as each season of their night melted into a sleep. Each time Musgrave woke, arrowy rain was still besieging the house. A caravan of dreams straggled confusedly through the room. It seemed to him that he was on an island surrounded by water and that, though his sharky sickness was out there behind every third wave, waiting to devour his breath and nose and windpipe and lungs, he was unshakeably secure while he remained on this patch of white-sanded dry land. The air of the whole sky from horizon to horizon shaped itself into a funnel: he had only to turn his face up and draw on it to swallow all air and ether everywhere.

She asked him, 'Is it true that you wrestle with your father's spirit when you're down?'

They had been forever asking him – women – and he had forever refused to reply: Now he said, 'I've a devil in me. It wracks at the sight of dead things and it won't tolerate me going near water. I take it for the devil who's washed away by baptism. My mother said that I was born in such a summer heat that the water in the font dried up in the hour or so it stood, and there was naught but a little gritty puddle that the priest made do with.'

'But you have good cause to fear water,' said Elinor, '–your father dead in such a way.'

He turned on his side with his back to her. 'I don't remember. I was four years of age; how should I remember?'

She reclined, watching his eyelids flicker with being shut too tightly, and did not say any more. She pressed herself – S against S – to the shape of his back and drawn-up knees, and the fire blew smoke out into the room and a log settled on the slab and flared up with a draught from under the door.

The moon stood out in the rain, grizzling, and lit little other than the wide Mole river. The currents plaited the water, and black, sinuous glides flexed themselves under the moon, and scrabbled the pebbles in a cattle drink.

'If I set you down here, you have a six-mile walk back and the way to find on foot.'

'You'll not get the horse across the river,' she said, but there was no note of triumph; it was just an observation.

'Don't mean to take the poxy horse over,' he said, pushing her off the animal. 'I'll wade over. Wait here for me and Barnard. We can take you back to see the mincing.'

Somehow he got out of the saddle, his legs offset. 'I think I'll maybe ask Barnard for you as a reward: Elizabeth Fettimore for a wife and enough gold to keep her in her high-and-mighty ways. I could, don't you think otherwise.' He looked from her to the horse with equal loathing and seemed to search about for something the darkness would not uncover to him. 'Something to break its legs with,' he mused, roaming up and down the bank.

'You brute pig!' she said, stirring her exhausted outrage. And she stood up and took the horse's bridle off and handed it to Geoffrey. He threw it as far out into the river as he could, then tried to shoo the horse away, but it looked at him contemptuously, wandered off a few paces and cropped grass.

He could not postpone it – the plunge into the river. She had been right about the rain raising it. Where in all probability Barnard and his men had crossed easily with all their shrinkables and fine clothing, on horseback, the water was moving fast, unbroken and incalculably deep. Perhaps this was the wrong section of river bank. Perhaps the ford was a mile to his left or his right, and this stretch was a bottomless rapid.

He had to forgo the cloak. He took his boots off, but the rocks on the foreshore hurt his feet and he put them back on, knowing he would need them on the other side.

He was trying to fix a face to the man who had told him that between this world and the after-life flowed a wide river guarded by dogs operating a ferry. When a fox began barking on the other side of the darkness, the whole concept became vastly plausible. He slithered down into the cattle-drink and stood for a while with the water running round his ankles. Surely those chips and debris that brushed against his calves were fragments of ice: the water was as cold as a glacier.

'Drown, you devil!' the Fettimore girl shrieked at him. She had the advantage of height, now, and the deeper he waded the more she seemed to tower over him, shouting, 'Drown you damned boy – you gross, vile, wicked, bloated, evil pig!' Thoughtlessly, he had let the chalk boulder drop as he dismounted, and when she saw it glowing on the ground in the dark, she raised it over her head in both hands.

He fell on his belly and swam, the rock falling harmlessly into the reeds.

The cold seemed to crack every rib in its jaws. The current swept his feet away wherever he tried to put them down, and although he paddled and flapped with his hands under his chin, it was only the buoyant blubber of his flesh that he relied on to sustain his soul, out of the clutches of trolls, ice floes, pike, weed, drowned men and this wicked, demersal cold.

He was grabbed from the water by a tree branch which might have caught him, like Absalom, by the hair but, lacking in hair, seized on his collar. For ten minutes he tried to find a way round its branches, pushed all the time into its wooden fork by the force of the swollen river. He could see Elizabeth watching him from the opposite bank, wishing that some tidal bore would sweep upstream and sink him once and for all. She was silent now. Everything was deathly silent except for the cracking of twigs and his involuntary grunts of cold as he laboured his way out of the tree and on to the bank. In the face of her contempt, it seemed hardly worthwhile to cry out at the scratchy pain and gnashing cold, so he climbed out speechless, past speech, and stood on the bank shaking violently from head to foot, looking back at her. His stance said, 'Hate me. I'm across now. I win.'

Her stance said, 'Next time the Jordan. Jordan's deeper and colder.'

She could see his palsied cold clear across the river. With the rain still leaning down on the black world, he would not be getting any drier or warmer before he found Barnard. She picked up the borrowed cloak from the ledge of the cattle-drink and wrapped it round herself, exaggerating its fleecy luxury.

Bracing himself against a tree to keep from juddering, Geoffrey spat in her direction, then squared his shoulders, peeled his clammy hair exaggeratedly off his cheeks to behind his ears, turned, took to his heels, and ran.

It was still barely four in the morning.

15

LIKE A CHALKSTREAM THROUGH the English hills, Musgrave's night repeatedly took him shallowly out of sight and delivered him up again clear and brilliant and sunlit above ground. He dreamed that he was flying over an open heath and that, far below, Elinor stood dressed in white linen, in a dip between two hills, swinging a lure and calling him by name. He stooped on her and paused in the air over her to take her head in his hands. But the talons he seemed to have in place of hands were tangling in her windy hair and he needed her help to extricate them. He woke to find Elinor's fingers interlocking with his. Pigeons in their loft below the end gable were just beginning to stir and mutter endearments to one another.

Barnard had had to rely rather heavily on rich pork and gallons of wine for getting his huntsmen to sleep. It had not stopped raining till four and they were all stretched out under gaberdines, most lying on their faces with the sheets held down at four corners with boots and fists. They were like a row of hides pegged out for drying by the sunrise.

There was no sunrise discernible — only a congealing of leaves on the surface of the day. Barnard did not trouble to wake at first offer.

He dreamt that his dogs had sprung a fine, tusked boar and that he was running it so close he could see its comical, bandy, stiff-legged gallop through the bracken ahead of him. He shot at it with a crossbow, and the barb stuck in its centre back; it stayed patiently for him while he searched through its bristles to recover his bolt. It had just died when a female boar, wearing a roasting spit through her body from nose to tail, minced out of the undergrowth and said, 'I'm St Friedeswide. Could I trouble you to tell me if my husband has passed this way?' Hoping to forestall her grief, he tried to stand in front of the dead boar, but she saw it, smacked her rubbery lips (only slightly inconvenienced by the spit protruding through her nose) and said, 'Chivalry's dead, I see. No matter. No matter. I've been disinclined lately. Have you perhaps seen the Lord Barnard around these parts?' And he had said, 'Who?'

'The Lord Barnard. Lord Barnard. Milord Barnard!' And he woke with the sound of someone calling his name urgently.

'Milord Barnard!' it called with a flatness that said it had called several hundred times already. Some of his men were awake, propped up on one arm, watching him from under their gaberdine.

'John Exton,' he said. 'Fetch me a face for that voice.'

Others went with Exton. Like beaters stirring up pheasant, their voices rounded on the voice and brought it out of the undergrowth in a flurry of cracking twigs. And Exton was confronted by a flat, frenzied, mud-caked Jack o'Green who stopped shouting at the sight of the huntsmen. It half-crouched, its arms angled in parenthesis round its body as though it was ready to fight any one of them, but it said nothing at all.

'You're one of Barnard's pages,' said Exton, his hand on his shortsword. 'Is something amiss at the castle?'

Geoffrey said nothing.

Here they were. In all the shaggy forest with all its million passageways, pits, snares, ditches and dark thickets, he had found Barnard's hunting party. They had not come far beyond the river. An hour before, he had found fresh dung from their horses and still not found them. But here they were and the dawn scarcely curded between the treetops.

His body was in limbo. Even to his own touch, his skin felt like a cold, smooth stone picked up from a river bed. If he did not move or speak, perhaps these men of Barnard's would lose sight of him against the clogging mud and rocks and bushes and tree trunks. Perhaps John Exton would come close, tap a finger against one staring eyeball and pronounce him vertical but dead.

Undoubtedly he was dead: it was simply another unforeseen injustice of God's that beyond the region of outer darkness, the place of wailing and the gnashing of teeth, there should be clearings of daylight like this to be endured. Was it beyond divine mercy to spare a man the ordeal of recollecting over and over again the series of events leading up to his death-by-freezing?

There were men here not beyond stoning adulterers to death. If he spoke now — the conviction grew in him — they would make him retrace all that path through the forest and the water and the open-land, and watch Elinor Barnard devoured like Jezebel by her husband's best brindled wolf-hound. These men here would enjoy the sport. These men here did not have their liege lady's cat-gut hair tangled up round an open wound of the heart.

Just then, Lord Barnard found his circle of followers and, in the centre of them, his foot-page Geoffrey, standing at bay.

'Geoffrey? I hardly recognised you, boy. Instantly! Is there trouble at home? Has any harm come to my wife? Exton, fetch

95

him a blanket and a swig of wine. Geoffrey, for the love of God, boy, speak!'

'Rise up and come away, master,' said Geoffrey, straightening his back, wiping his face with his sleeve.

('If I can see none of them,' reasoned Geoffrey covering his eyes with his shirt sleeve, 'they are none of them here. I've told no one.')

'Must I shake it out of you, boy? Are you waiting for money?'

'Rise up and come away, master. You're wife's in bed with the Little Musgrave. If you wish to watch their sport, sir, you had best come straight away and catch them at it. As I've done. As I've done. I've done, I've done.'

Barnard's blow lifted Geoffrey off his feet and he landed on his back at young Furleigh's feet.

'Lord, master Geoffrey, how did you fly!' said the simple boy through his cleft palate. But his father grabbed his arm and pulled him away. He could see Barnard sink for the spring, like a dog back on its haunches.

It was nobody's place to restrain Barnard from killing his own foot-page. He restrained himself in the end, when his fingers were tight on Geoffrey's throat. The boy put up no struggle. It eased none of Barnard's fury to wring this neck or stop up this mouth: the words were already out — like the world's sin out of Pandora's box.

Profound indifference wandered into Geoffrey's eyes: he did not get up even when Barnard climbed off him and walked away.

'It's a lie, of course,' said John Furleigh — not to his liege but loudly enough to be heard by him. 'Some scheme by this boy for money.'

'Yes!' said his son, enthusiastically, not understanding but

96

discomforted for his father by the lack of cheery assent. The rest were too appalled to speak. they were not appalled by the accusation (such a little fault) but by the power it had to bring down the lieger. However low their link in the feudal chain, such a shaking of it at the head would in turn shake them. The axe had hit the tree at its roots, but the leaves shuddered at the blow and knew that they would dry and drop if the damage went deep.

Barnard himself, like the termite queen, tasted in his saliva that, on some far-off rim of his intricate empire of joy, an intruder had broken in and that decay, however far away, would break down the hill fragment by fragment and that the taste in his mouth would worsen until he could taste nothing but destruction.

'If it be true,' he said, standing at the edge of the clearing with his face turned to the forest, 'you'll have your gold, Geoffrey.' (All the derisory birds were starting to whistle at him: see-what! see-what! weep-you! weep-you! poor-fool! poor-fool!) 'If it be lies, you had best hang yourself like the other Judas, or I'll surely draw and quarter you in my lady's sight.'

To add confusion to dismay, Barnard left them all standing in the clearing and, stepping over a log, walked into the forest. Its profound shadows swallowed him so completely that it seemed he had stepped out of the window of a high tower and fallen into the obscurity of a green abyss.

Only John Exton went to Geoffrey where he lay, resignedly, on his back, staring up at the sky. Exton extended a hand to the boy to help him up. 'You're cold.'

Geoffrey looked back with the dumb accusation of an animal in the stock pens, singled out by the slaughterman. 'I'll none of you. You're a friend to the Little Whoremaster.'

97

'Musgrave?' said Exton. 'I don't drink or eat or keep acquaintance with goats, master. Musgrave's nothing to me. He's a dead man, and I wish no better than to see him graveless.'

Musgrave dreamt that he was swimming in a glass goblet of wine, and that through its walls he could make out a marriage feast with drifts of white flowers overblown on the table. It was the wedding of Elinor to George Barnard – and the bridegroom too drunk to see that there was broken cork in his wine – that Musgrave was bobbing against his lip at each mouthful. Several times the swimmer called out to him: 'I shall poison thee, Barnard! Your wife concocted this poison!' But Barnard (his eyes set in his skull and a saddle over one arm whose stirrups kept tripping him up) opened his throat and swallowed the last dregs – Musgrave and all. And Elinor said, 'I am innocent. I am innocent of everything except sin.'

16

As FAR AS THE RIVER, the pace was killing. Barnard (when he re-emerged with the look of one who had harrowed hell in the few minutes allowed him) rode out at the head of the column, his huntsmen straggling behind him. Sliding and weaving between the trees, the horses broke from trot to canter through clearings and bundled together in a confusion of kicking and half-unseated riders where they were forced back into single file. Even as they squeezed their riders between trees, there was no conversation, only the occasional swearing under the breath as another man caught the wet slap of a leafy branch in his face. Each man watched the horse in front, its flanks swaying, its tail breaking like a column of water over its fetlocks, and he ducked and leaned in the saddle and pulled in his torn gaberdine and cursed and imagined the scene in Barnard's head — that's to say, the scene in that warm upstairs chamber at the manor-house.

Exton and Geoffrey fell in together at the rear of the train, Geoffrey protected from Barnard by the long chain of mounted men and protected from the thought of him by the all-consuming preoccupation of staying astride the horse they had given him. Exton had the reins in his hand, which brought the animal so close to the tail of the forward horse that Geoffrey was in constant peril from its kicks.

Better accustomed to horses, Exton could direct some energy

to thinking. Even back here, he glimpsed occasionally the grey shavings of Barnard's neck and tried to discern from the stoop forward over the pommel what thoughts were breeding in his head. In looking back to check that the foot-page was still aboard his horse, he glimpsed, too, Geoffrey's face and asked himself time and time again what financial reward could make all this worthwhile. Becket's murderers could have expected more gratitude for their work than this miserable wretch.

'You must hope they are still about it,' he said, as the frenzied trot broke to a walk and Geoffrey barged to a standstill beside him, clinging to the mane. They had reached the river. The boy's voice was contorted with pain at bouncing uncontrollably in the saddle the whole way. 'You must wish them still about it, boy.'

'I heard you, milord,' he said, transferring his head to the other side of the horse's neck, away from Exton. 'I wish them both dead and forgotten and things to be the same as they were.'

'That won't be so for you, now. Whole or quartered, that's for certain,' said Exton dismounting. 'No. You wouldn't be a "made-man" but for the Little Mandrake and his indiscretion. Don't worry. We shall sprinkle him with blood since that's the treatment mandrakes cry out for.'

Because he did not expect to see contempt in one so far beneath him, Exton discounted the look on Geoffrey's face as mere pain. 'It amuses you, sir. I can see that.'

Poor fool, thought Exton – not to take joy even in earning his blood money and to live in dumb bestial ignorance of the damage he inflicted on other people. Brute peasant stupidity – like that welter of flesh – cushioned his soft, inward parts. It would be different for George Barnard, as it was different for

Exton himself. Geoffrey, edged like a blunt spade, was luckier than his sword-edged, sharp-honed betters.

The first horse, head bent back, nostrils flared, eyes white, was being led through the river.

'This is not the same place,' said Geoffrey. 'This is not the ford,' and then at the fresh memory of the cold, 'Must I go through the water again? Can't I stop here?'

'Why?'

'It terrifies me,' he said. 'After my coming here, the water terrifies me.'

'How did you get here — eight or ten miles? On foot? On a pitch-moon night?' But Exton was not interested in the answer: he was contemplating all the civilised 'sensibilities' Musgrave had purported to have. Gentility to the ladies, passivity towards the men, a herbivore among ferocious, bloody animals. This hygienic, sweatless animal whose no-sweat set real men ill-at-ease, had wrapped himself cheerfully in the stench of venial sin. Insensitive to the feelings of the only *good* woman to have loved him, he had managed to debauch Elizabeth without even lifting her skirts.

Elizabeth. He thought of how the news would break in her tomorrow like an hour-glass. All the fragile vessels that hung inside her — vessels which could be kept intact: which a good husband would have striven to keep intact — would break. Disillusionment, bile, contempt, revulsion, disgust would pour down and swamp her picture of Musgrave and overflow into a hatred of all men, that they could behave so bestially. Exton, unless he could recommend himself to her quickly, would be swept away along with manhood in general. And all because of Musgrave's insatiable appetite.

Well, he would lay claim to her through her uncle — as

Barnard suggested – and bide his time until the Little Mandrake had rotted in the earth of her memory, and he could recover males their reputation for civilised behaviour. In any event, he would have her. The only rival in his path had shrunk already to a bloody patch on Barnard's sheets – a thing as easily broken and forgotten as virginity.

'I took a horse from the Fettimore house,' Geoffrey was saying, 'and the woman Elizabeth along with it. Another of Musgrave's conquests. She was minded to warn them, so I carried her with me as far as the river – out of harm's way.' At the look on Exton's face, Geoffrey began to explain again, trying to be more lucid. 'Warn them. She was going up to the house to warn them. But I left her by a deeper crossing than this, I know. It would go badly with me to lose her – though she can walk back now it's light, that's true.'

'Exton! Exton!' Barnard's voice across the water was distorted into a sound like bitterns on the marsh. 'D'you seek to delay me, John Exton? I'll not wait for you or that dropsical swelling with you,' he bellowed, and Exton plunged into the river and the cold, as he clung to his horse's saddle and crossed the current, froze all thoughts and sensations for the while.

In his mind, Barnard had reached the chamber threshold for the thousandth time. The tread on the seventh stair creaked for the thousandth time. The large door on its leather hinges stood in front of him and his hand was on the latch. Sometimes when he opened it, his valuable, imported linen sheets heaved like the cloth over a basket of adders. Sometimes, as now, his wife looked up from the window seat with a look of pleasant surprise and set aside her book of hours or her embroidery and said, 'Did the rain drive you home, my lord? Let me fetch you a cordial and rub you warm. I fear I turned off Geoffrey while

102

you were gone, for all he's Scrivenor's son, but he was just too ...'

'John Furleigh,' said Barnard. 'Come up alongside if you please.'

The column set off again before Geoffrey had got clear of the river or Exton had remounted. The pace, though, was not the headlong gallop the men had been expecting now the way ahead was open.

'Furleigh, I must protect my good name, you know, against this quat, this delinquent of mine; still I don't doubt but my lady's honest.'

'Of course not, sir. Her virtue's a matter of common ...'

'So I see no purpose in stumping home like a pack of Vandals. If things are as they should be ...'

'I don't doubt it, milord.'

'... If things are all at peace, Furleigh, I see no need to outrage Elinor, my wife, with military manœuvres under her window. D'you understand? There's no need for her to take it amiss, us coming home early.'

'I'll tell the men, sir.'

'No galloping the horses through the very gates — it's bad for them, eh? — No damn swords or bloodletting.'

'Perhaps you would prefer to go up alone, sir?' Furleigh suggested.

'H'm. Perhaps. Perhaps.' But on the thousand-and-first imagined ascent of the stairs and opening of the leather-hinged door, Elinor raised her head from Musgrave's chest and winked at her husband, wetting her lips, while Musgrave toasted him derisively with a raised glass of wine. 'Oh, Furleigh. While you're telling the men,' he said, 'say that the horses feet are to be clothed. And no voices raised within a mile of the castle.'

'And no horns to be blowed, milord,' said Furleigh, attracting his lieger's unspoken hatred by his look of profound, cow-eyed sympathy, 'albeit we are coming back from the hunting. Supposedly.' He patted the horn that lay curled in the crook of his leg, and Barnard wondered if he was the butt of a cuckold joke, too, as well as an object of pity. He said, 'No horns, Furleigh. No horns of any kind.'

He looked beyond Furleigh, down the line of his men. Was there not one there to whom he could say the words which kept rising in his gorge, so as to be rid of them? Was there no one who would lean across out of their saddle and incline a discreet ear to the words, *I did so love the Lady Elinor.*'

Furleigh brought back the word as far as the river bank. After he had gone, Exton let the column draw away from him until they were out of sight. Geoffrey was incapable of mounting without help, hopping on one foot, his weary legs barely answerable to him, his horse answerable to no one so inept.

'Help me up, master,' he said, as Exton pulled his dripping horse round by the head and came close. He went on hopping; Exton had not moved from his horse's side.

'Let me satisfy myself of something, Geoffrey,' he said. 'Did I understand you to say that you brought Elizabeth Fettimore out to the river, by force, and left her there all the cold night long with the rain coming down and no shelter from the cold and no way to protect herself from wild animals or the like of you? You stranded – abandoned – a woman of quality to further your plot for advancement?'

Geoffrey stood still beside his animal; it stood between them shivering with cold, and Geoffrey could just see over its saddle into Exton's face. 'Heaven's windows are dirty, then,' he said peaceably as Exton drew his shortsword. 'Joan used to say that, you know? When sinners prosper and the righteous fall, then are Heaven's windows dirty. I don't think it was a gipsy saying. I think she forged it out of her new acquaintance with windows at the castle. If you kill me and Musgrave's found whoring, you'll be taken for his friend and defender. If you kill me, it won't make the woman Fettimore better than she is. Could have had her myself if I'd had the mind.'

The suddenness of Exton's attack startled the horse, and it leapt aside, knocking Geoffrey off his feet. The slash of the sword cut through the patch of air where his head had been and struck the animal squarely across the throat.

It rocked on its four feet, forward, back, to right, to left. It tried to bite Exton, but its teeth clamped shut on nothing. It breathed in through the base of its windpipe – a chesty, hollow gargling, then coughed and dropped on its front knees, subsiding into a gentle, open-eyed sleep on the ground. Exton stared down at it.

When his legs would hold him, Geoffrey stood up and turned his back on Exton to face the river (it also saved him the sight of the horse). 'Your lady was warmly dressed, sir. And mine was not a plot for advancement. It was purest hate, the sort that's in you now. I could wish that hate didn't sap a man's energies so.' Despite the weariness, he could not help but twitch a little at each alternate second, anticipating the pain of Exton's shortsword through him.

'Don't speak!' said Exton, apoplectic with disgust. 'If I have to share a horse with you, I don't have to listen to you. Christ Jesu, boy, it's a fine man you've brought down.'

'The Lord Barnard. I regret it sorely.'

'Barnard. Yes. Him too.'

17

BARNARD'S TRAIN PASSED A WILD, wet woman by the stone circle of monoliths not two miles from the village. She was sitting with her back to one of the stones and a cloak pulled round her knees and feet. With her hair plastered by rain to her face and neck, she looked no better than a gipsy girl and perhaps one abandoned even by her own kind. Those at the head of the train rode right by her. One or two crossed themselves at the sight of the immobile little figure with its face turned down. They wondered whether to check if she was dead, but she stirred then and sank her face on to her knees; they turned back into the line. Lem and Oswald saw her too and exchanged words. Apart from the straggler Exton and the fat foot-page, they were bringing up the rear. They looked furtively over a shoulder, slowed their horses and drew over towards the stone circle. The girl put her arms round her head and did not look up.

The horses edged closer until Lem and Oswald were looking down the length of their manes at the girl. Again they exchanged grinning glances and Oswald lifted a leg over his pommel to dismount.

Over the crest of a rise, Exton with the bulging, treacherous little foot-page behind the saddle, came within hailing distance of the train for the first time since the river. Oswald settled back into his saddle and he and Lem pushed on hard to catch up.

It was Geoffrey and not Exton who recognised Elizabeth first, but he stayed up on the horse while Exton dismounted.

'And has Barnard made you rich, boy?' she said, her little voice raw and full of phlegm.

'Rich as I had hopes for,' replied Geoffrey from the great height of the horse. 'Are you well, madam?'

Exton was chafing her hands between his, rejecting every thought that came to him like a girl on her knees looking for four-leaf clovers. It was not long before he felt the line of communication between Elizabeth and Geoffrey cordon him off.

'Did you give up, or change your mind, that you stopped here?' asked Geoffrey.

'I saw the train coming a long way off,' she said. 'I knew you had won.'

'Won?' said Geoffrey. 'Won.'

She turned her head towards Exton as though he were someone whose name she ought to know. 'Do you understand what's been happening?'

'I know,' said Exton, 'but understanding's something different. Musgrave's a seducer and a devil. He paid his feu by bringing down Barnard so low he can scarcely move. The man's undone. Let him burn.'

She looked him piercingly in the eye: 'I can hardly do otherwise, can I, John? But I do still love him. My soul's tied to him like two witches tied up for drowning. As he sinks, so I'll sink, too. Down and down. It was no more than self-saving to try and preserve my Little Musgrave.' Exton began to bluster like a loose sail in a wind, but she cut him off. 'There's no way you don't understand, John Exton. For if you haven't loved me at all, I've seen your regard for Robin since I can first remember. Ah, he's a maypole.' This eluded Exton entirely. 'I've been sitting here thinking since I saw you all coming. He's like a painted maypole. Women twine him in their sin and men twine him in their envy like a maypole. But a maypole's just a pretty thing in itself, with its ribbons loose.' Her sigh was an expression of universal disappointment. 'Lord God, how I do love him still. A respite from it would be a mercy. I swear, after they cut him down, I'll never dance at another.'

When Geoffrey tipped himself forward into the saddle and successfully urged the horse into a trot, Exton jumped up, shook his fist and shouted after him. But Elizabeth laid a restraining hand on his ankle and said, 'Let him be. There's venom enough in that lad to murder Musgrave a hundred times over: I don't know why. But it's only natural he should want to be in at the kill. We simply have to walk a mile or two, that's all.'

'Take my arm, lady,' said Exton. 'You would do me honour by walking with me to the warmth of your house. There's no heat in the day.'

They walked to the brow of the next rise – the heaths were wave-form and crested – and could see the chain of horses diminishing in size towards the village. Beyond them it was no more than a little wall painting on the plaster-coloured sky, with the green mould growing up to its base and daubs of cloud threatening to obliterate it from above. In the foreground, Geoffrey perched on a horse which turned round and round on its own axis, nipping at Geoffrey's boot with its long yellow teeth, the reins dragging between its legs.

Elizabeth clapped her hands together and relished the spectacle. They both assumed that the horse was out of control; Geoffrey punched at the neck of the saddle in obvious frustration and then his head dropped down as if he was in tears. But when he saw them coming he brought up from among the thick locks of the mane Exton's hunting horn – one hung on each saddle flap – and put it to his lips. No sound came except a wet squelch and a breathy wind. They came closer and still he blew into it until his colour began to change.

'Please, master,' he sobbed, 'it makes no damned sound. Doesn't it work or something? I've turned myself inside out and it won't make no sound!'

'It's a matter of pursing the lips,' said Exton, in a detached, remote voice. Geoffrey tried again. The spit burst from either side of the mouthpiece and the horn gave a small, vexed groan.

He threw it down at Exton's feet. 'You blow the bugger. I'm near ruptured. You blow it!'

Exton bent and picked up the horn, a look on his face as though he were Ceres finding the Cornucopia all empty and spit-filled on a midden. 'Why? Why should I? Who for?' he asked with a kind of bewildered apathy.

'It's what your lady wishes!'

But Elizabeth wore the look of a condemned prisoner tormented by her executioner with a momentary stay of execution: renewed hope was a renewed ordeal. Exton looked at her and found that his breath was tight in his chest with loving her. Her vulnerability reminded him of Musgrave when, in the throes of his falling sickness, he had lain in Exton's arm's. Somebody was trying to cut out Exton's lungs and lights to make Musgrave whole again and he thought perhaps this woman had made the first incision and asked him to continue the operation himself. But he could not blame her. Ironic when so much breath was needed to blow a horn that his windpipe should close down and his lungs fill up with passion. He was going to sink Musgrave if he did not master the situation and take a good, deep breath ...

The blast from the horn set hoops of metallic air clanging and jangling and growing in ever-spreading circles. It made the horse — unnerved by the stranger on its back and the horn-sound shivering out of a man on foot — take off at a gallop. Geoffrey clung to its mane for an age-long ride — even as far as the next crest where the animal barged sidelong into George Barnard's grey and skittered on past him. A second double-blast made Elizabeth cover her ears and boomed back off the plaster walls of the sky. Barnard turned back, scattering his train of men.

'John Exton!' Barnard's shout was crushed by the third blast: he was still far off. He rode down the slope, rode through the sound of the horn; rode right up to the two on foot and wrenched the horn out of Exton's hand. 'John Exton, I turn you off. Take yourself out of England. I destitute you. Why, man? Disinherit your children? Wreck your good name? God damn your soul if you've damned me to unknowing. But why?'

So Exton was the first leaf to fall after that blow to the roots. One moment he was green and sweet, and the next the sap was cut off and he was dry and falling and falling into a darkness reeking of mould.

'Give me a reason, lad. Give me a reason!'

Exton raised his hands and let them fall, waiving his right to defence. Elizabeth slipped her cold hand into his and the rain returned suddenly in big, splashing drops.

'Love of a friend, milord,' he said, chafing Elizabeth's hand between his own. But Barnard's back was turned: divots of wet earth flew up round them as the grey stretched itself. It had shed the cloths around its hooves.

18

THE VILLAGE WAS BEGINNING to wake up; its animals were making petulant conversation, demanding each other's attention. Cows overburdened with milk recollected their calves angrily. Goats splayed their thin legs not to be over-balanced by their swinging milk, and bleated uncomfortably. Sheep bawled at one another from under their soggy fleeces. Some sodden cock, though it had held off till now, began making a tally of men's overnight sins – three crows to each household and a symphony of reckoning for the big house.

'Maiden,' said Musgrave. 'It's daylight.'

Elinor's feet stirred as she walked down the flowery cloisters of another intricate dream, but she did not move from his chest.

'Elinor,' he whispered. 'I have your maidenhead. What will you say when you're asked for it?' She whimpered in her sleep and answered him in a wordless language like the mouth-music of the old western gipsies. He said, 'I dreamt that you sent me to buy dispensation from the Holy Father and that when I reached Dover they said that, with such a quantity of gold, there was no more room aboard for me and if I wished to cross the Channel I must walk. And I walked clear across from Dover to Calais without ever missing a breath and the water was full of fish but all the fish had wings, and you stood on the jetty at Calais waving ...'

'What are you chattering about, my lover?' said Elinor, pushing up off his chest. She came from the other side of sleep like an Arab infidel turning his face into a hot, dry wind, mouth pursed and her material hair hanging across her face. He saw the pupils of her eyes contract as though she was falling away from him through fathoms of space. But after a second they dilated wide to swallow his soul.

'I was asking if you would close with me once more, lady. It's almost time to rise.'

'I pray God Barnard will never come back,' she said fiercely, 'and that we can stay here for ever. In this bed.'

'We should soon starve.'

'What? With Little Musgrave made entirely of honey?'

'Then I should soon lose my wits, lady, for you're surely saltwater and sailors run raging mad who drink saltwater.'

'Why am I saltwater, master Mariner?' she asked obligingly.

'Because the more I drink of you the more of a thirst I have.' And the saltwater and honey combined into a sweetwater burn tumbling strenuously and urgently all the way from the Garden of Eden through a desert to its confluence with the River Jordan.

Out of the hostile territory of the Hittites and Perizzites and the Amorites and all those others usurped by Musgrave's coming out of his desert — one long, shrill blast came from a single horn. Two more followed it, with all the stridency taken out of them by distance — a mile, maybe two.

'It's Barnard's huntsmen,' he said peaceably, as if to reassure her as she flinched in his arms.

'It's nothing but a goatherd shouting out. Barnard will be gone these three days.'

'Perhaps we have been here for three days and the moon kept the cover pulled up for kindness' sake.'

Elinor did not smile but seemed to be trying to press herself under the lip of his body like a crab, at the shake of footsteps along a beach, creeping under a rock. 'I'm cold, Robin. I'm bitter cold.'

Raindrops cracked on the window and eaves, each one like a poppyhead exploding to expel its cloud of seeds.

'No, lovely person, there's no time to make you warm. Barnard will be calling for his breakfast presently and you surely won't serve it to him in your shift?'

'It was *nothing*,' she repeated. 'I've set young Geoffrey to watch for Barnard and he would tell us at once if anyone ... Must you make excuses to leave me, Robin? Your hawks are fed and your horses watered and there's a fire in your grate. Don't take it from me, lover, your fire.' Her nails dug into his arm. 'For Christ's sake, stay with me an hour or so more. It's bitter cold.'

He stroked her hair and shushed her as he had seen mothers do with their babies, letting the love whistle between teeth and lips. 'I want no more lady. Just let me see that Geoffrey's not asleep, and breathe in the rain, and I'll return me to your bed and ... there. There's such a weight of sleep upon you, lady. A man might creep under it and be out of the cold completely. Let no moths eat it into holes before I come back, now.' He slipped out of the white pool of sleep she spilled across the bed and went to the door.

So repelled was he by the idea of a voyeur beyond the door that he was almost relieved to find no foot-page on the landing.

Nor on the stairs. Nor in the great hall. From the head of the staircase he could hear the main door banging in the wind. When he went to close it, he saw his leather jerkin hanging beside the dead fire and a spillage of cotton smock from the fireplace.

Before fastening the door, he went outside on to the lift bridge and looked at the furniture floating free in the swollen moat and the ducks riding out the storm aboard a trestle ark. They quacked at him, scandalised by his nakedness out-of-doors. He looked out across the heath to where the hawk she spoke of hung by its feet in the bird-catchers' nets. Riders were straggled across the farthest bluff like fleas crawling towards the tenderest, most bloodfilled parts of a sleeping giant.

The rain trickling down his naked back made him shiver uncontrollably. He secured the door, carried the clothing back up to the landing and opened the chamber latch as quietly as possible.

Elinor stirred marginally at the touch of his cold, wet skin and said, 'It was nothing but a shepherd boy.'

'It was nothing, madam. Nothing much. Sleep on. We'll close in the morning. When the sun is up.'

The fear was so tight at the base of his neck that little blooms of colour kept bursting into flower behind his eyes. He eased his chest from under her hand so that the beating of his heart would not wake her. His legs' sinews stiffened repeatedly at the imagined run between the house and the stables, between the stables and outlawry; leaving behind Elinor immured by the furnished moat, her treacherous servants, the bloody sheets.

'Do you know,' he said when she seemed about to struggle like a mayfly nymph through the meniscus film. 'I've never slept between sheets before. It's an uncommonly soothing thing.'

And she sank back into the green water of sleep with her wings still folded.

He heard the tread of hooves on the lift bridge – a muffled exclamation – a few puzzled whispers suppressed into silence. And then it seemed as if a remembered dream filled in the space between terror and blind panic. He had been standing in the Temple with an unseemly quantity of gold, bartering for an indulgence with the seraphim when, suddenly, one of them took wing and bore down on him with the tongs from off the sacrificial altar. No, neither were they tongs but a pair of swords in a double scabbard, both of which the angel drew and plunged with relish into Musgrave's chest.

At the foot of the bed, the Lord Barnard drew aside the bed curtains and showed a head caked with mud, rings of white round his eyes and morsels of pork hanging in his beard. His receding grey hair was spiked with wet and dirt, and water trickled off his gaberdine on to the covers. Musgrave thought he had never seen a man so weary or so mortally wounded.

'I said, how do you like my sheets, Musgrave?' His voice was tied down with so many chains of restraint that Elinor did not even stir in Musgrave's arms.

19

Musgrave shielded Elinor's ears from his own voice.

'Well enough my lord. I like them well enough. But I like your lady wife a world more. If your sentiment for her was ever the like of mine, you won't wrack her with fear the moment she wakes. Withdraw, sir, I beg you.'

Barnard opened his mouth once, then twice, but no abuse could he hawk up to void over Musgrave. A residual astigma of love blurred all shapes in the room except his wife's head on Musgrave's arm. Sin ought to have slimed it like stagnation in a well. Sin ought to have made some visible claim, stamped some repulsive seal on her. Lucifer ought to be scaly by now and ashen-mouthed and not snatch at the heart of mortal onlookers as she hurtled down through the abyss.

Barnard did not withdraw. He only snatched the bed curtains closed so that the rings screeched on the rail and a cloud of dust burst out of the dirty brocade. Beyond the curtains Musgrave could hear the tinkling of buckles, the drip of gaberdines. He kissed Elinor on the mouth, and she woke with a smile.

'Maiden,' he said. 'I'm pressed to leave. Pay me your best attention.'

'It's *nothing*, I tell you.'

'Well, it's very little, but I would be grateful for a glimpse of your eyes.' She frowned at him and the drip, drip, drip of the gaberdines seemed to fill the room. 'We are honoured by the company of your husband and some other worthy gentlemen. It would be discourteous to leave them standing. They must be weary.'

How he had hoped she would keep from screaming, knowing how it tightened the resolve in a huntsman's stomach to hear the boar squeal and knowing how it weakened his own. But she was such a child; it was optimism misplaced. He and Barnard found themselves on opposite sides of her, holding her either arm, as though she was the hysteria neither of them could quite master. Musgrave could see opposite the reflection of his own face in Barnard's flinch at each penetrating scream. His other hand reached out – and so did Barnard's – to pull up the sheet and cover Elinor against the relentlessly impartial eyes of the huntsmen.

'This is dire, milord,' he muttered. 'Let me accompany you to the landing and be done with it. For decency's sake, I should have liked to die with my breeches on.'

Between them, Elinor subsided to whimpering, and turned her face in to Musgrave's chest. The unconscious preference recovered and redoubled the rage in Barnard who, out of sheerest temper, rended down the side curtains of the bed and flung them on to the floor. It drew off the eyes of the others who, transfixed into one corporate being, followed the fall of the curtain into a dust-smoking heap beside the door. Musgrave saw their heads move as one and the universal stoop of the neck, the universally half-open mouth, the universal start when Barnard shouted:

'Get up, young man! Get up as quick as you know how! I'll not have it spread about that I cut down a man without sword or weapon but, by God, my sword aches for you!'

117

'Fight you, sir? Fight *you*, sir? I've no sword.'

The spectators began making sounds of approval at the lieger's noble gesture. Barnard was filled with contempt for them, for their predictable lip-licking relish at the thought of sport — a cock fight, a gladiatorial brawl, a scrap between two pedigree dogs. Musgrave was filled with bitterly ironic amusement; to him it was simply a matter of dying in the rain rather than here in the comparative warmth.

Sparing Elinor distress, and winning that great span of life that stretched between the bedroom and the courtyard were the only two thoughts in favour of confronting Barnard with a sword. He had a bad enough conscience about wishing *not* to spare Elinor anything. He did not want to be the unbacked cock torn to bloody shreds to the delight and cheers of a biased audience: he wanted an ally — a faint cheer from behind the chorus of derision.

He looked into Elinor's face for signs of some powerful character trait on which he could lean in place of courage. Her face said, to his appalled dismay, 'Kill him, my lover. Fight him, with me for the prize. This is our great chance.'

Barnard was saying, 'I have a new pair of Italian swords — two blades in one scabbard. You can take one and I'll have the other.'

Musgrave gave a sort of ribald cheer and laughed out loud, shaking his head, and Elinor crouched up on the bed and said, 'Take it, Robin. Kill him with it!'

Barnard slammed the door with a crash Musgrave supposed to equal the sound of a man's heart breaking: his laughter sobbed to a halt. He took Elinor's shoulders between his hands with a paternal gentleness he could only attribute to the instant ageing of his soul. 'Sweetest lady. I've a mortal fear of dying — mortal, ha! – a coward's fear of it. This last night has lessened it, but not so much that a brave man could tell me apart from a craven rabbit. Feel here. D'you feel how I'm trembling? Just like the rabbit. If you were counting on me to free you from your lord and husband, I do wish I had opened your eyes sooner so you could select a fitter man for a champion. I'm no man for a sword fight! I negotiate with my horses whether they turn or run straight! I don't fill the clothes my father dressed me in,' he said, as he pulled on his shirt and trousers. 'I'm a man out of my station. You need to feel a man's better or at least his equal to make him bleed, and there's no man born low enough I would consign to that dark place I'm so afraid of myself.' Her eyes eyes were glazed. There was still that stiffness of her cheek muscles and flattening of her nostrils and downturn of her mouth that made her face a warlike thing – as if it was armoured in one of the old Roman helmets. Nothing but blood would assuage her. 'I disappoint you, mouse,' he said. 'Very well. I'll go and fight Barnard. God knows, I'm a younger man and he's weary as death – I may strike a lucky blow and carve myself a barony.'

She was content. Better than content, she was overrun with images of victory-snatched-from-defeat. She was saturated with the certainty that everything would turn out for the best. Musgrave put on his clothes to the accompaniment of her plans for their future and her avowals of a thousand years of love.

'Where are my boots? Were they put beside the fire, too?' She could not remember. The future laid claim to such a quantity of boots that she could not muster concern for a single extant pair.

'I'll go and find them, lady, and return directly. Will you get dressed for me?' He wanted her away from the context in which

119

Barnard's anger might be kept alive, fed by possibilities to the point where he would kill her too. 'Kiss me, sweetheart, for my legs not to shake in front of my neighbours.'

She hung on his neck as they kissed. The goodbyes of women, thought Musgrave, are liked seaweed that drags a drowning man down when he most needs to be buoyed up. 'You'll come back to me the instant you have your boots?'

He prised her arms from round him. 'I must find them first. Be patient.'

Shut the door. Put the woman out of sight. Obscure the mirror of himself with all its terror and unfounded optimism and unfulfilled youth and parcel of promising happiness. Yes, it was better without the reflection in front of him. It was easier to believe that if he held up a mirror now to his face, the glass would be empty. If he had blessed her, she would have known he was not coming back. Well, God could bless her if He chose: Musgrave had lost all influence in the matter.

He turned from the chamber door where his forehead had been resting for some time to find the foot-page Geoffrey holding out his boots to him.

'They were outside, beyond the moat, and they're wet.'

Musgrave wondered if this was a source of satisfaction to the boy, but he was glad enough of a reason to sit on the stairs and pull on the boots, even though they were leaden with water. 'It was your work, was it, all this?' No answer. 'No, I'm sorry, boy. It was purely my doing. I know it. Tell me, Geoffrey, who blew his hunting horn? Was it an idiot or a friend?'

'John Exton blew it,' said Geoffrey.

'Ah, My dear, good John. God love and prosper him. Will he suffer for it?'

'He's banished the country – so the others are saying. Why do a man's doings spill over into other people's fortunes?' said Geoffrey, but the self-accusation was wasted on Robin.

Musgrave smiled. 'Are you preaching to me, boy? It's a little late. Jesu bless and save me, Geoffrey, I don't seem to be able to use my legs.' He grinned sheepishly up at the boy's dough-like, expressionless face. 'It's the wet in the boots, you understand.'

Geoffrey gave Musgrave a hand up and felt that dystrophy of terror usually kept secret by the discreet, hardened executioner or hangman.

On the courtyard, George Barnard stamped about in the rain, banging the cold out of his limbs, banging the thoughts out of his head. Soldiers have that facility.

Musgrave came out of the glow of the house-door and a funnel of wind lifted his hair and filled his shirt. Stiff-legged, he looked as though he was wading through the rain which had covered the entire yard with a pitted, jumping shine.

He stopped side-on to Barnard, holding him not to be there until he was looked at, and he breathed in the unrepeatable scent of rain. Rain: it had fallen through fathoms of grey sky, been turned off the wings of flying birds, had absorbed the smoke of a damp charcoal fire, splashed off the trembling leaves of webbed and worm-eaten trees, sunk into the sweet, bark-strewn ground, been sucked at by white-flowered magnolias, had bled through the veins of the soil to a river. It had been drunk by fish, savoured with sea salt, strained through the sails of sunken ships and drawn up again through white sieves of surf into the golden bowl of the sun until the clouds broke it out again as this cold sweat. Musgrave could smell each inch of its journey. He breathed deeply again.

121

'I hear you're afflicted with a sickness,' said Barnard coldly. 'Will it prevent you fighting?'

'No, sir,' Musgrave replied. 'Apparently I'm afflicted this morning with nothing but terror. – You'd expect no better from me, would you, sir?'

The swords were in Barnards hands. He did not seem to have found the scabbard. He offered the handle of the longer sword.

'My reach is longer, sir, if anything. You wrong yourself.'

'All the same, you shall have the longer. In front of witnesses. You'll not impugn my honour any more than you have already done. What, still wanting to talk, canary?'

Musgrave poked the words at Barnard through the railings of rain. 'I beg you to recall John Exton. If you exile men for their acts of foolishness, France'll soon list, and England ride a fathom higher in the water.'

Barnard levelled his short sword at Musgrave's head. 'You don't plead for my strumpet wife, I see. Too busy joking.'

'I wasn't joking about John, sir. Your wife needs no defence. You surely know I took her by force and all without gentleness or her encouragement? You've only to hold her reputation up alongside mine to judge her kindly.' Musgrave looked down the length of his own elegant sword. It shone keenly even now with the sky so dark in the face that it seemed to have been taken by the throat and choked. The sword tip gouged moss out from between the stone slabs and flicked it across Geoffrey's feet. 'Ah yes,' said Musgrave, grinning with the startled recollection of a joke, 'Geoffrey's standing up for me. My second. He'll be second to you too, if you like. Second to everyone, that's Geoffrey. Sorry, boy. Pique should be beneath even me. I just can't be rid of this wretched fondness for being alive. Go

122

off and present my abject regards to your mistress.' More moss flew and the sword twanged.

'In a while, sir. I'll stand up for you first,' said Geoffrey quietly, and for a second or two both men stared at him.

'Put up, Musgrave!' Barnard yelled suddenly, and the whole courtyard echoed it, distorted it and boomed it back at them. 'For God's sake, man, defend yourself!'

'What? Against the indefensible?' Musgrave's sword stood diagonally across his body. As Barnard's lumbering rage came in on his chest, Robin moved his sword hand across as if to parry and deflect the tip. But he dropped his hand, his sword tip swung down between their feet and, for a moment, he stood with his arms slightly spread.

The sword entered just below his sternum: he thought he saw, as Barnard withdrew it, the black, stringy shape of a shrew-sized devil impaled on its tip. He looked Barnard in the eye, cocked his head – as to a fellow conspirator – and would have commented but for the uncommon lack of words at his command.

20

THE SPECTATORS WERE AGGRIEVED; Musgrave had robbed them of a spectacle. Fitzsimmon clapped respectfully, tapping his fingers on the palm of his other glove and when the rest scowled at him, said, 'Well, it was a well-placed stroke!'

Above the courtyard the gallery window opened with a clatter and Elinor Barnard leaned out amidst a cloud of hair, her shift sleeves trailing down past her fingertips. The rain was falling so hard that it was impossible to look up into it and make out her face – only white flapping like a seagull, and a wild breaker of hair.

Barnard rapped Geoffrey's arm and, in a low voice, said, 'Tell her Musgrave's words. If she don't glory in it ...'

Geoffrey pushed through the dripping rows of men, pushed past the cordon of steely rain and clattered through the door. The draught curtain made a grab at him but he fought it off and ran across the great hall to the staircase. The rake of it clutched at the sinews in his legs and back, he fell up it and barked his shins; he seemed to be climbing into a higher zone of more gruelling gravity, his ears crawled forward on his head to strain after sound of Elinor's screams. Or abuse. Or tears.

'Lady,' he hissed, flailing into the gallery passage. 'Come away, lady. Come away!'

She remained cruciform and leaning forward, her hands on the handles of the wide-open shutters. He could glimpse under her arm the white and brown shape of Musgrave darkening in the puddling rain.

There was no time to waste in persuasion; at any moment she might burst into the same clamour of screams that were aching in his own chest. In a hissing whisper, he let the reprieve stream out in words barely separate.

'Little Musgrave says he took you by force and the master's wanting to believe it, but he can't if you show grief and you've got to rejoice over his dying or he'll have your life too less'n you can save his face in front of Furleigh and the rest but he's so inclined towards you he won't believe ill of you if he's a shred of a chance not to – and why have more people hurt than need be? Isn't it enough for him to be gone?'

She withdrew from the window and turned a face to him so pasty and mask-like that he hardly recognised her. For a seventeen-year-old she might have been forty. She said, 'It's you.'

'It wouldn't mean anything and there's no use in grieving when your life depends on it. It's only for show and to help Barnard out of losing face.'

'You skinful. You midden. You grub. How did he come dead? He was young and fit and quick.'

'He put down his sword, ma'am. He leaned on to the blade. It was right quick for him.'

'You Judas. You grubber.'

'Did you hear what I said, lady? Barnard won't kill you if you just fall in with Musgrave saying he took you by force.'

She seemed to acknowledge the idea for the first time. He could not do more and he wanted to be out of the sight of her and out of reach of her hatred which had leapt into the cradle of his soul and was clawing up its newborn face.

'My love to your ladyship,' he said catching her wrists as she flew at him, forcing her on to her knees and crouching down himself. Love to the whore and love to the angel. 'Love to the Lady Elinor Barnard and *may she live a long life*.' The last words he emphasized with twists of her arms that threw her in close against his chest. 'For Jesu's sweet sake, won't you save your soul long enough to take you past next eucharist?' The stiffness went out of her and he let her go. 'Won't you do this little much to stay alive?' he pleaded.

'And be at your mercy ever after?'

'What?' The idea had not crossed his mind. A boy from the service end and the Lord Musgrave's lady? Such thoughts had not entered his head for how long! For a year? For only a day?

'I shall take myself to France with John Exton if he lets me.' The seventh board of the staircase creaked. 'Your husband's coming, my dearest love. Remember. Nothing will avail Musgrave now.'

He stumbled off down the corridor wiping his eyes and nose with his sleeve and stepping aside out of his master's way. Barnard stopped him passing, with a hand on his chest.

'You surprised me today, Geoffrey,' he said with an unlikely conversational tone. 'I never knew you to be so subtle. It's ten gold pieces for the news and another two for that piece of gentility in the yard. Quite the imitation of a gentleman.'

'Your wife's waiting for your comfort, sir. She's been put to a fearful ordeal.'

'Ah, a politician! Yes I understand you, Geoffrey boy. Well, let's see. Where is she?'

Swaying towards his wife along the ill-lit corridor, his sword under one arm, he peeled off his gloves. 'Well, lady? How goes it with you? How comes my furniture in the moat?' he said to the Lady Elinor who sat on the floor of the gallery. She looked up at him with eyes as moved as Bethesda, and he gave a great surrendering groan and sat down too, in his redoubt of gaberdine and mud and rain. Reaching out to cup her face in one hand he managed a smile. 'How goes it with you, Elinor?'

'Faith, can you find me a lady more wretched or more abused, my lord? I don't believe you could in all England. Why did you leave me alone — unprotected? Everything's undone. Everything's spoiled.'

'I'm living and your ravisher's dead. Is that "everything undone"?'

'Tomorrow it may be enough. Today there's no heart in me to breathe or stay alive.'

'Oh, I think there is, my love. We do all cling to life in the end, no matter what. Oh, except that rabbit in the yard. He bolted down the closest hole, he was in such a hurry to be down in hell.'

'I can smell his fur singe now,' she said, fixing her eyes on her husband's chest. As he watched her listening for the cock crow, he recollected how sympathetic a fellow St Peter had always seemed in his paltroonery, persecuted by that relentless, nagging bird. 'What should I do with his body, do you think? The decision's yours. Come down and give the word to the men who are left. Whatever you decide, we'll do.'

She raised angry eyes to meet his and then let them slide back down his face to rest vacant near his mouth. 'Must I look at the creature again? It's not gentle for a lady to see dead things. You ask a lot.'

'But I do ask it, Elinor. Come and let the men see you spurn him.'

'*Spurn* him? Of course I *spurn* him, George.'

They went downstairs, not touching, she a skirt-length ahead: he wanted to rest an arm round her shoulders but this time it would have betrayed his own vow made for the protection of his own sensibilities. At the foot he said, 'Your laces are undone, madam. You can't go out like that.' She paused and he put her hair forward over her shoulder and pulled up the cords – and her figure appeared like shapeless snow melting over the outlines of a shrub.

'I have no sleeves. Do you wish me to fetch them?'

'No.'

'Green's an unlucky colour. Do you wish me to change it?'

'No.'

'The rain's fearful. Shall I not wear a cloak?'

'Of course, my love. You mustn't catch cold.'

Beside the door she put on her cloak and drew up the hood – just as Geoffrey might have drawn up his imagination. Inside it the sounds and faces of the courtyard seemed more remote. She understood why a blinkered horse was pacified. The world was at one remove. It signalled to her dumbly from the other end of a tunnel – a family of ducks standing on the lift bridge, the lording Fitzsimmon with his gaberdine stretched round the shoulders of the young Furleigh boy, the pig-run in the angle of the walls, the men's faces stirred out of a sodden boredom by a late chance of excitement. They memorised each movement she made: their wives would want precise details. The funnel of her deep hood let in pictures of the streaming flag-stones edged with moss, and then gradually encompassed Musgrave's body – boots, wool hose, codpiece, a shirt transparent in the rain and his face ...

'What is it, Elinor?' snapped Barnard clamping her arm in his hands to curtail the shriek.

She turned right round to him so that she could see his face in her hood's opening. 'You could have shut his eyes.'

'I hadn't noticed. They were of no importance to me.' He raised his voice. 'Say what shall be done with the body, lady.'

Inside her hood, Elinor said, 'It should be treated with Christ's grace and charity. It's foolishness to take revenge on a man's body when he's no longer in it. His soul's already at Judgement. You were wrong to bring me here.'

Barnard stripped back her hood, which was baffling her voice and blinding her good sense. 'But shall he have his pretty body for the Resurrection, say you – a body that's violated so many good Christian women?'

It was harder without the shelter of darkness, the sharp rain driving through her hair, picking at her skull. It was harder when she could see all the big, brutish hands white and half-curled around the courtyard like the landcrabs that gather round a drowned man to tear him to pieces. She could not speak.

'Tell me, lady. How do you like his face now there's no deceiving smiles about it?'

She liked it well enough. How unconditionally beautiful he had been, with his almond-shaped, dark-lashed eyes and cheekbones like the leading arch of an eagle's wing, and the alien corn of his short-cut beard where she had gleaned such bushels of love.

'How d'you like his body now, now it can no more pleasure you?' He had picked up Musgrave's sword, or rather his own, long, Italian rapier, and was toiling uphill towards rage.

'Poor George.' She could see he was so tired that his body almost refused the climb. She knew it as if it were an incontrovertible law of nature, that the less she lied, the more beautiful she became: she would have liked to spare George that. But there was Musgrave to consider, and such a long way to go before she could equal his beauty. 'The body's near as lovely as when my Robin was wearing it, Barnard. He's dearer to me empty even, than you and all your estates and all your damnable family.'

'No priest?' said Furleigh as Barnard put the sword up to Elinor's breast.

'Not here, milord!' someone shouted as he drove it through her heart.

'On the heath, milord,' someone shouted as he withdrew it.

'Or her ghost'll haunt the place,' someone whispered involuntarily as the second stroke went home.

'Was dressed in green like a fey,' said a voice as the third and fourth slit the velvet and the white cotton shift began to show through each slash red, red, red.

21

WHEN GEOFFREY REACHED the Woolwich Ferry, the ferrymen were chocking the wheels of Exton's cart on board the wooden platform. A string of other carts was queuing to board, but would take only half an hour to load. He was glad to arrive with so little time in hand. The press of people and the panoramic spread of houses beyond the river would have cowed him had he not been goaded on by his schedule. There must be a hundred dwellings in sight at one time!

Still, his anonymity was reinforced by every face. In the village he had been a bad smell in every nose – he had received more attention from his neighbour's backs than in all his unnoted life. But here he was restored to anonymity: he tried to draw on it and on the merits of his journey.

John Exton and Elizabeth were standing at the wooden rail, looking across the river. He called out but the thunder of horse and bullock hooves on the hollow raft drowned his voice. His horse was pushing itself forward between two carts. It was not intentional but he expected, by the moment, one of the thick-necked, flat-headed farmers to swear at him and beat him back to the end of the line. They did not. His new steward's clothes marked him out as instrumental to some lord above them in rank. However long they had waited, they made way.

'Hold my horse, boy,' he said and pushed along the jetty. 'Lord Exton! Mistress Exton! Look up!' Elizabeth narrowed her

131

eyes against the glare of the river. 'Your ban's lifted, sir. Bar-nard's sent to recall you.'

Exton leaned out over the rail. 'My land?'

'Yes, sir. Restored, sir. But he says he won't help you to Miss Fettimore and he hopes her uncle forbids it.'

'Doesn't he know we're already married?' said Elizabeth.

A woman newly married should smile more, thought Geoffrey – particularly at the sound of good news. Perhaps she had contracted that same paralysis of the cheek as he on that wet, bitter night – a stab of cold to the brain's nervous core that left the eyes a little vacant and the facial muscles immobile. There was animation left in Exton's face, at least.

'Will it be tenable, do you think?'

'What's that mean?' said Geoffrey.

'Will our neighbours stomach us?'

A two-horse dray was being loaded aboard. There was furious commotion when Exton intervened, waving his hands and telling the ferryman that his cart must be unloaded. The queue had milled forward to the lip of the ramp and a dozen animals between traces had to be reversed. The animals on the platform stamped and rolled their eyes uncomprehendingly at efforts to back them on to dry land again. But the farmers and merchants did it. They did it for the cut of Exton's clothes and the breed of his face. Geoffrey noticed how they stored up the expletives till Exton's cart was off, turned and pulling away.

'Where can I sell this horse?' he asked Exton as a cabbage was shied by an anonymous hand and bounded harmlessly in on top of the baggage. Exton reined in and the thrower of the cabbage crossed himself and hid.

'Are you the owner, Geoffrey?'

'No,' he replied. 'I'm stealing it. At least I'm stealing the

132

money I get for it, for the animal was given into my charge for the purpose of bringing you back.'

'And are you breaking your bond, boy?'

'That's right, sir. I have twelve gold pieces, a new suit and the price I get for the horse. I'll take ship for France and buy a field and put pigs in it.'

The two looked at him, expressionless.

'I like pigs. They keep their eyes on the mud and never look up. And when a big fat boar needs a leg-up, I can help him to it, can't I? And be richer for it after.'

There was a pause he could not fill, then Elizabeth said, 'Change your money with the ship's captain, or you're sure to be cheated.'

'Here are three gold pieces for your horse,' said Exton. 'I'll sell it before we reach home. Sleep on your pack, and don't play dice with the sailors, d'you hear, boy?'

'Yes, sir.'

He climbed down, and tied his horse to the tail of the cart. It clattered away towards the drove road, Exton and his wife sitting wide apart at either end of the driving board, the cabbage bobbling about between the legs of a chair.

Shortly, it and the jetty's end both receded to a speck, and the grey mudflats sloped up on either side, like the back tendons of a rotting, unburied giant down whose sweaty spine the ship crawled out to sea. Two days earlier, Geoffrey had not believed life to be — what was the word Exton had used? — tenable? But he had been exaggerating, as usual. The Plague would have taken more and left less, and given him worse dreams. The vacant hole where his imagination had once transmuted lead into gold had caved in, collapsed, been filled by a fall of earth. But a man breaking his feudal bond, sailing towards a field of

133

foreign pigs and a country awash with an incomprehensible language had less call for imagination than he had for sharp wits, a short memory and a fat, thick skin.

He sat down well inboard of the rail, on a bale of fleeces, and held his pack between his knees. Inside his shift, the green velvet sleeve slipped down and rubbed softly against his white belly. He began to whistle softly, to give himself heart, and a passing sailor, mistaking him for a scurvy foot-page in the failing light, slapped him in the mouth and asked if he didn't know it was bad luck to whistle aboard ship.

As it fell out upon a day,
As many in the year,
Musgrave to the church did go
To see fair ladies there.

And some came down in red velvet
And some came down in pall;
And the last to come down was the Lady Barnard
The fairest of them all.

She cast a look on the Little Musgrave
As bright as the summer's sun;
And then bethought the Little Musgrave,
'This lady's heart I've won.'

'Goodday, goodday you handsome youth
God make you safe and free;
What would you give this day, Musgrave,
To lie one night with me?'

'Oh I dare not for my lands, lady,
I dare not for my life;
For by the ring on your white hand,
You are Lord Barnard's wife.'

'Lord Barnard's to the hunting gone
And I hope he never return.
And you shall sleep into his bed
And keep his lady warm.'

'You nothing have to fear, Musgrave;
You nothing have to fear.
I'll set a page outside the door,
To watch till morning clear.'

And woe be to the little foot-page,
And an ill death may he die.
For he's away into the green wood
As fast as he could fly.

And when he came to the wide water
He fell on his belly and swam;
And when he came to the other side
He took to his heels and ran.

'Rise up! Rise up, Master!' he cries
'Rise up and speak to me!
Your wife's in bed with the Little Musgrave:
Rise up right speedily!'

'If this be truth you tell to me,
Red gold shall be your fee.
But if it be lies you tell to me,
Then hanged you shall be.'

'Go saddle me the black,' he says,
'Go saddle me the grey,
And sound you not the horn,' says he,
'Lest our coming it should betray.'

Now there was a man in Lord Barnard's train
Who loved the Little Musgrave,
And he sound his horn both loud and shrill,
'Away, Musgrave! Away!'

'Oh I think I hear the morning cock,
I think I hear the jay.
I think I hear Lord Barnard's horn:
Away, Musgrave! Away!'

'Lie still, lie still, you Little Musgrave
And keep me from the cold.
'Tis nothing but the shepherd boy
Driving his flock to the fold.

'Is not your hawk upon his perch,
Your steed is eating hay.
And you a fair lady in your arms,
And yet you would away?'

So he's turned him right and round about
And he fell fast asleep,
And when he awoke Lord Barnard's men
Were a-standing at his feet.

'And how do you like my bed, Musgrave,
And how do you like my sheets?
And how do you like my fair lady
That lies in your arms asleep?'

'Oh it's well I like your bed,' he says,
'And well I like your sheets.
And it's better I like your fair lady
That lies in my arms asleep.'

'Get up! Get up, young man!' he says.
'Get up as quick you can.
For it never shall be said in my country
I slew an unarmed man!'

'I have two swords in one scabbard –
Full dear they cost my purse.
And you shall have the best of them,
And I shall have the worse.'

So slowly, so slowly he got up
And slowly he put on;
And slowly down the stairs he goes
A-thinking to be slain.

The first blow Little Musgrave took,
It was both deep and sore.
And down he fell at Barnard's feet
And word he never spoke more.

'And how do you like his cheeks, lady?
And how do you like his chin?
And how do you like his fair body
Now there's no life within?'

'Oh it's well I like his cheeks,' she says.
'It's well I like his chin.
And it's better I like his fair body
Than all your kith and kin!'

And he's taken up his long long sword
To strike a mortal blow,
And through and through his lady's heart
The cold steel it did go.

As it fell out upon a day,
As many in the year,
Musgrave to the church is gone
To see fair ladies there.

Traditional